A MALI HOOPER THRILLER

#DANCEFEVER

KADY HINOJOSA

BOOK 3

TITLES BY KADY HINOJOSA

THE MALI HOOPER THRILLER NOVELS
#HuntedLives
#JusticePrevails
#DanceFever

Join my mailing list and get monthly updates
on new releases, special deals, and more.
www.kadyhinojosa.com/s

For my Mom, who always supported
me and cheered me on,
no matter what I wanted in life.
Although she is no longer in this earthly realm,
I know she continues to cheer for me
and to encourage me to reach for the stars.
She would love to have read my books.
Thank you, Mom!

CHAPTER ONE

Cobble Hill, Brooklyn
Monday, December 20, 3:35 p.m.

ON A BITTER, icy day, pimply-faced, fourteen-year-old Jimmy Archer died in his bathroom.

One hour earlier…

"Hey Jett, it's here!" exclaimed Jimmy after his best friend answered the call.

"The candy you ordered? Man, that was fast."

"I told you that candy app I found was cool, better than Amazon. And this candy is special. You gonna come over and have some with me?"

"Nah, Mom was sick and didn't go to work today. Gotta stay home with her. Besides, she'd kill me if I ate that crap. Your mom would do the same to you. You know how they're on that health kick."

Jimmy grimaced. His buddy was right. His mom didn't allow him to have any candy except the zero-sugar crap she gave him on occasion. It was nasty. So he was a little pudgy. He was fourteen, a teenager, and should be able to make his own decisions. Even his grandma said the baby fat would melt off as he grew up. His mom went way overboard, always insisting he eat carrots, celery, and other shit like that, and she was always embarrassing him in front of his friends, smacking his hand if he reached for a cookie at a party, or telling him he'd only get fatter if he continued eating doughnuts and cakes. She really pissed him off at times…which made this candy order all the sweeter. He chuckled to himself, pleased with his catchy humor.

"She'll never know."

"Right. Until she gets the credit card bill. My mom goes over every expense on her bills to make sure she's not getting ripped off from anyone."

"Not mine. She spends so much money in one month, this little order will go by unnoticed." Jimmy laughed. "Are you sure you can't come over? Mom won't get home for another hour or so."

"Wish I could, man. Tell me which candy you liked best when we play *Forge of Empires* later. We're still on for seven, right?"

"I'll be there. Later." Jimmy hung up and turned to the brown box sitting on the dining table. He licked his lips in anticipation as he used some scissors to cut through the tape. Peeling back the lid, he laughed in delight as a whiff of sweetness assailed his nostrils. He stuck his head inside and inhaled through his nose as much as his lungs would allow, then pulled back and flipped the box upside down. Jolly Rancher gummy bears, cherry lollipops, PEZ sticks, chocolate bars,

Starburst candies, and other delectables tumbled out, littering the table in a colorful array of savory treats.

Jimmy rubbed his hands together, trying to decide which one to eat first. He pushed his stringy hair back from his face and scratched his pimply cheek, considering his options. Finally deciding on chocolate, he opened a bar and shoved it into his mouth, sucking the chocolate and groaning in delight. Eyes closed, he rubbed his belly as he swallowed, cracking up for pulling the wool over his mother's eyes. Smacking his lips, he opened his eyes and lifted his arm to wipe off the chocolate that had dribbled down to his chin. He swayed when he looked down at his windfall. As a result, he had to grasp the chair in front of him with one hand. Reaching toward another treat with the other, he paused and frowned when he noticed the time.

Deciding that he should hide all evidence in case his mom came home early, he piled everything back into the box and raced upstairs to his room. As he walked inside, he gazed at all of the Anime. He loved everything Anime, and his room was plastered in it. Posters covered the walls with every character, and his sheets and bedspread were a colorful rendition of Demon Slayer. He kicked off his Anime tennis shoes and hung his Anime backpack on the desk chair as he walked toward the bed. His room was an explosion of color and he loved it all.

He jumped from one foot to the other as he peeled off his Anime socks with one hand and tossed them on the floor, then plopped down on his bed and opened the box again. Closing his eyes, he reached in, rustled around for a few seconds before pulling out the next sweet he planned to gobble down. It was a small bag of Jolly Rancher gummy bears. He smiled. Perfect. Tearing it open, he poured them into his hand, selected a red bear and a green bear, and popped them into his mouth. His eyes widened as a myriad of flavors invaded his mouth. Heaven. With eyes closed again, and a dreamy look on his face, he tipped his head back and crammed the remaining bears into his mouth, chewing and sucking on them, giggling as warm juice trickled past his chin and down his neck.

Suddenly, his eyes flew open and he stopped chewing as a wave of dizziness struck. Without warning, he leaned over and puked repeatedly. Small chunks of gummy bears and chocolate liquid slid down his bedspread and formed a puddle on the floor. He staggered to his feet and stumbled to the bathroom. Looking in the mirror, he wondered, in a detached sort of way, why his lips were blue before he gasped and sank to the floor, his back against the wall. His body stiffened and he started to shake, and his breathing became more labored. Gurgling, he continued to gasp for air, struggling to breathe.

Sixty seconds later, Jimmy died.

* * *

Special Unit Warehouse
Undisclosed Location, New York
Tuesday, December 21, 6:45 a.m.

She stepped out of the elevator and shivered. A svelte five foot eight, Agent Mali Hooper was a force to be reckoned with. Those who assumed she was delicate and all fluff—given her privileged life growing up in the Hooper dynasty of Philadelphia—and was nothing more than a pretty face, soon realized their mistake. Her unusual almond-shaped gray eyes reflected intelligence, kindness, and a toughness that surprised even her at times. Many likened her to one of her favorite actresses on Hallmark because of her eyes, flawless skin, youthful appearance, and athletic physique, a compliment she actually liked. They were the same people who typically underestimated her. As a Tactical Intelligence Analyst for the FBI, Mali was part of an elite team tasked with solving cases surrounding social media murder crimes. She loved being on the team and felt they were all part of a family.

The cavern, as the team had affectionately started calling their control center, was always cold. Not surprising since it was located three floors beneath Henderson Deliveries, a front for the task force started by her fiancé and fellow agent, Jacob Black. Located in a nondescript warehouse in a warehouse district inside New York City, they had been operating there for four months or so.

Mali walked into a large open space with a conference table, chairs and multiple whiteboards on one side, and the restrooms, vending machines, and security monitors on the other. In the middle was a white high-standing table, the glass top of which was the technical control center of their operation, an IT specialist's dream piece of equipment. Computer tables with multiple monitors on each were placed in front of the control center leading toward the back. The focus of the room, however, were nine large screens mounted on the back wall, three across and three down, that could be used as nine individual screens, one large one, or anything in between. The control center operated them, with data easily displayed by a simple swipe of the hand across the table top.

Mali was not the first to arrive. Joe Alters was ramping everything up as she walked in. She had no clue when he arrived each day but he was always there before her.

"Okay, where is it?" she asked with a smile.

Joe looked up from the screen. "Hey, Hoop. Where is what?"

"The cot that you sleep on. I'm beginning to think you live here." She smiled as she walked past him and set her purse at her computer station.

Joe laughed. "What can I say? I love my job."

"Yeah, you love playing with that control center, you mean."

"Well, there is that."

Mali laughed as she turned on her computer and prepared to start the day.

"I beat him, right?" Kirsten Bellows, an IT specialist and Mali's good friend, sailed into the room and high-five'd Joe as she walked by. She stopped next to Mali, out of breath. "I was going to call but figured you'd be here early."

Mali shook her head and smiled. "I don't know when this little competition between you and Jake started…"

"…yeah, you do. Jake started it, at no prompting from me I might add. He called me an amateur!"

Mali giggled. "Ah, so he didn't start it, he just challenged your sense of friendship and honor."

"Damn right he did. I couldn't let that go unanswered, of course, which is why I started calling you earlier." She sighed. "Well, did he?" She set her things down at the computer station next to Mali's.

"I hate to break it to you, but yes. He called as I was walking into the building."

"Damn him! I knew I should have called instead of waiting to get here."

"You do recognize that you won't be beating him anymore in eleven days."

Kirsten sighed again before she looked at Mali and smiled. "I know. And I will gladly give up that particular challenge on New Year's Day when I witness your marriage and happily ever after. Can you believe you're going to be a married woman in fewer than two weeks!?!"

Mali's look softened as she stared off into the distance.

"Hello? Earth calling Mali." Kirsten snapped her fingers in front of Mali's face, laughing as she did so.

Mali blinked and, blushing, grinned at her friend. The two had met during FBI training at Quantico and, despite their different career paths and background, had become fast friends. She often compared Kirsten to a bulldozer, her stocky build, average height, and go-get-em-and-get-out-of-my-way attitude lending Mali to that comparison. Mali oft-times wished she could adopt that 'I don't give a damn what you think of me' attitude. "I pinch myself two or three times a day. A wife and a mother. I feel so blessed."

Kirsten gave her a quick hug and said, "You are, honey, you are. And so are they! Jen and I are thrilled for you."

"Let's do a zoom call with Jen and Sara today at lunch."

"To finalize the plans? We're still leaving in the morning, right?"

"Yes."

"I'll set it up. Is eleven-thirty all right?"

"That works. Thanks Kirsten."

They both settled into the morning routine as other members of the team began to arrive.

Mali turned on her favorite news live stream, WABC, on her second monitor and began to read her e-mail on the primary monitor as she listened to the morning news.

"In case you're just joining us," said the reporter, "fourteen-year-old Jimmy Baker was found unresponsive in his bathroom by his mother when she returned home from work yesterday afternoon." A picture of Jimmy was displayed on the screen. "Pronounced dead at the scene in upscale Cobble Hill in Brooklyn, his body was taken to the morgue where an autopsy will be performed. An open package of gummy bears was found on his bed as well as a box with a variety of candy. It is believed he ingested some which may have been tainted. As there was no return address on the box, the origin is unknown. All candy has been confiscated by the DEA and will be tested. His mother was unaware that her son had obtained the sweets since he was forbidden to do so. We will update you as soon as we receive more information."

Mali stared at the picture of the young boy. *How sad. Gone too soon, and devastating for the family.* Now that she was going to be an instant mother in eleven days, stories like these stuck with her and frightened her. Being a parent was such a huge responsibility and she didn't have nine months to mentally prepare herself. Jake had proposed to her less than three months ago. They had decided on a short engagement, much to the consternation of her mother, because, well, why not? They weren't getting any younger and didn't want to waste any time. It was also a calculated move so she could have an intimate wedding instead of one with five hundred guests, as her sisters had to endure. Mali chuckled and shook her head. *Still a rebel.*

"That looks like a devious smile." Jake squeezed her shoulder as he stopped at her desk.

Mali looked up at him, her expression softening as she took him in. She'd never get tired of looking at him and being with him. Jake's muscular physique complimented his dark, smoldering looks. She always thought of him as a panther, just waiting to pounce. His jet black hair, intense blue eyes, and the thin scar on the left side of his face lent a dangerous air to him. She wasn't surprised when she first met him and discovered he was in special ops for the Army for fifteen years prior to taking an early retirement. His skills and knowledge were ideal for an FBI field agent, and now head of their task force. "Just had a vision of my mother running to and fro trying to finalize details for the wedding."

Jake gave her a look.

"Don't look at me like that. She is in her element when under pressure, despite what she says. She's just relieved that I'm finally getting married. They both are."

"If anyone can pull off an intimate society wedding in less than three months, it's your mother." He smiled. "Are you all set for tomorrow?"

"Kirsten and I are zooming with Sara and Jen at lunch today to finalize things."

"Good." Jake perused the room. "Everyone is here. Let's get our morning meeting started. It's a short week."

"Shorter for us," Kirsten chirped when she heard Jake's last comment.

CHAPTER TWO

Heading to Philadelphia
Wednesday, December 22, 7:15 a.m.

"YOU ARE GOING to spoil us, Mali," stated Sara, as she leaned back in the plush seat of the stretch limousine, beaming with pleasure. "I can't believe how much space there is inside." She ogled everything with interest. A mini bar and small television were just two of the accessories that captured her attention.

"You mean my father is going to spoil you, and you deserve it by the way. He insisted on it so we could talk unimpeded and without the stress of driving in this weather and traffic."

"Well I, for one, am going to give him a huge kiss when we get there." Jen snuggled next to Kirsten on the opposite side of Sara and Mali. All four burst out laughing at the image evoked by Jen's comment. While Mali's friends had never met her parents and sisters, she had spoken of them over the years.

Mali wiped tears from her eyes. "I look forward to seeing that, Jen." She smiled as she reached into the ice chest she had brought and pulled out a carafe of orange juice and a bottle of champagne. "Mimosas anyone?"

"Oooh…definitely," stated Jen.

Kirsten leaned forward. "Hell yeah."

"I'm glad none of us are driving. Count me in," added Sara.

Mali grinned. As she poured each a glass, she reflected on the special friendships with her BFFs.

Mali met Sara, her oldest friend, at a summer camp when they were just ten years old. They clicked immediately and had grown closer over the years. Sara always fussed over herself, self-conscious about her weight and what she called her frizzy red hair. Mali wished she had more confidence in herself, frowning as she watched Sara tug her shirt down and try to tuck her hair behind her ears with her free hand. Sara was the most steadfast of all of them, was married to the love of her life, and had three beautiful children who were her pride and joy. She was a mama bear and no one messed with her family. Mali was the godmother of her three kids, a responsibility she took very seriously.

Jen was Mali's college roommate. She was a rising star in her field of event planning and Mali was thrilled she was getting the recognition she deserved. She worked long hours and had an eye for detail, like Mali, that served her well in her job. Standing five feet ten, Jen was often compared to Marilyn Monroe. She was sophisticated, gorgeous, and dripped sexuality. People were drawn to her like moths to a flame.

Mali had introduced Jen to Kirsten and the two

had been together for more than three years now. They were total opposites. Jen was an extrovert and Kirsten was more comfortable working on computers; Jen was tall and willowy, Kirsten was average height with short, cropped dirty brown hair. She would laugh if anyone tried to refer to her as being dainty. But the two clicked and that's what counted.

"A toast." Mali raised her glass and the others followed suit. "To my best friends, you are more than I ever imagined I could have when I was growing up."

Champagne glasses clicked as her BFFs cheered. "Hear, hear!"

Talk during the drive was animated and full of laughter as they chatted about the wedding and wedding night, the honeymoon, and life in general. Mali's sides hurt from laughing so hard as the limo got off the interstate in Philadelphia.

"We're almost there."

"Has anything changed since we zoomed yesterday?" asked Kirsten.

"No. As Mother confirmed last night, we have an eleven o'clock appointment for the final fitting of our dresses. We'll go to lunch followed by the cake tasting. Mother also plans to stop by Riehs Florist to make sure all designs for the floral arrangements and bouquets are set. When we get home, I want to show you Mother's gardens and where the wedding will be held. I'm sure we'll have time to do that before dinner." She looked at her watch. "We should have enough time to go up to our rooms and freshen up before the day gets started."

Sara asked, "When we spoke yesterday, you said your sisters might be there."

Mali shook her head. "It's difficult for them to break away during the week. It's probably for the best."

"I was looking forward to meeting them," said Sara.

"It will be just the four of us and my parents. Tomorrow morning, we'll have a leisurely breakfast before heading back to the City."

"We'll be on the road by ten thirty, right?" asked Jen. "I'm working with a new client and have a two o'clock meeting at their office."

"We should get back in plenty of time."

Jen nodded her thanks.

As they turned into the property and drove up the long, winding driveway, everyone exclaimed over the beauty of everything. The house, built with gray brick, was typical of the Victorian era. It had a large porch, bay windows, and five tall chimneys. Multiple spires rose up toward the sky and were capped by a red tiled roof. Dark red shutters framed the sides of all upper floor windows. Majestic intricately-carved double doors, painted the same red, beckoned one and all inside. It was beautiful in the spring and summer when the grass leading up to the house was a deep green, and hydrangea and other flowers, as well as the trees lining the drive, were in full bloom. In winter, with trees bare of leaves, the plants dormant, and the grass covered in snow like a white carpet pointing the way to the house, it was imposing, stark, and yet, equally as spectacular.

Not one peep from her friends. Looking at them,

Mali smiled. Their faces were plastered to the window like little kids with their mouths hanging open.

"Better close your mouths, ladies, before bugs crawl in and nest there." She laughed.

"We can't help it, Mali. It's gorgeous," murmured Kirsten, her awe-struck voice barely heard.

"I can't believe you grew up here!" exclaimed Sara.

Mali shrugged. "It was nice in some ways, not in others. Here we go."

The car pulled to a stop and Roger, the butler, approached the vehicle and opened the door.

* * *

"Jasmine, darling." Willow floated down the staircase as Mali and her friends walked inside. With hands outstretched, she pulled Mali in close for a hug. Leaning back, she smiled. "You look lovely."

Mali squeezed her mother's hands. "Thank you, Mother. I want you to meet my friends." She turned to her BFFs and made the introductions.

"Your home is amazing, Mrs. Hooper," enthused Sara.

"Thank you, Sara, but please call me Willow. All of you." Her tone changed to one of business as she continued. "Ladies, Jasmine will show you to your rooms. Please make yourselves comfortable. Let's meet here in the foyer in…" She checked her watch. "…one hour. We have a busy day ahead of us. I'm off to make a few phone calls. I'll see you soon." And just like that, Willow walked away, disappearing into a room.

"Your mom is gorgeous, Mali." Jen watched Willow float down the hall. "Or should I call you Jasmine?" She grinned as she glanced at Mali.

"Don't you dare!" Mali exclaimed with a laugh. They started up the stairs. "Only my family calls me Jasmine. My parents were quite dismayed when I changed my name even though, as I told them, *Mali* means *jasmine* in Siamese."

"Well, the apple doesn't fall far from the tree. You take after your mother." Mali cocked her head to the side, lips pursed, as she glanced at Sara. "And Jasmine is a pretty name," she said. Mali's face cleared as she smiled her thanks.

"I understand why you decided to change it, though. You were quite the rebel, weren't you?" joked Kirsten, admiring the artwork as they climbed the stairs. "These paintings are amazing."

Mali didn't comment as she turned down a wide hallway at the top of the stairs. Her friends were taking everything in, talking non-stop until Mali stopped at the first door. Opening it, she said, "Kirsten and Jen, this is your room. You have your own bathroom. Sara's is next door and my room is the last one on the right at the end of this hall." Everyone walked inside.

Decorated in soft, soothing shades of gray with the scent of lilies permeating the air, the large room sported a king size bed on one end and it faced an electric linear fireplace on the opposite wall, where blue and orange flames danced inside the glass. A small round table with two chairs were positioned in front of a large picture window overlooking the gardens on the side of the house. Fresh lilies were in vases on the table as well as the nightstands on either side of the bed. The room evoked a sense of peace and encouraged its occupants to take a deep breath and relax.

Jen spun around, slowly taking everything in. "This is the most gorgeous bedroom I've ever seen! The details in the crown molding and furniture…wow!"

Kirsten, whose mouth had hung open since walking in, nodded enthusiastically.

Mali smiled. "I'm glad you like it. Mother renovated the entire house two years ago. Some of the bedrooms didn't have fireplaces so she added the linear style for additional warmth and coziness in each room." She pointed to a closed door on the same wall as the fireplace. "The bathroom is through that door. Let's meet downstairs in about twenty minutes and I'll show you around the house before we leave. Please, make yourselves at home. Come on, Sara, I'll show you to your room."

"Thanks." Kirsten waved in a distracted manner as she continued ooh'ing and ah'ing over everything around her.

Mali walked to the next door and opened it. Both walked inside. While the room was identical to the other in terms of furniture, fireplace, and picture window, this one was bright and friendly, decorated in pale yellow and rose. The scent of roses filled the room and a vase of roses sat on the table. It was a cheery and serene room.

"Mali, this is perfect," exclaimed Sara as she turned in a circle, absorbing all she saw.

"I knew you'd like this room. It fits you."

Sara reached over and squeezed Mali's hand then turned and walked to the window. "I imagine the gardens are lovely in the spring, although with the snow they look peaceful."

Mali joined her and looked down on the snow-covered grounds. "I always loved Mother's gardens. They are her pride and joy. You'll have to check them out from my room later. The windows overlook the gardens at the back of the house, where the wedding will be held."

"This has been an eventful year for you, with the Hunted Lives game and the whole deal with Janet Simpson. Now marriage. How are you doing? Excited about what's to come?"

Mali sighed. Sara was the most grounded of her friends and always cut to the chase. "When I started working for the FBI, I never imagined I'd be directly involved in any case, much less a life-or-death one with the game. And when it became personal with Janet Simpson and my father's partner...that was surreal. Doing intel from a computer or phone for an upcoming case is not the same thing, not even close."

"Do you still like working for the FBI?"

Startled, not expecting that question, Mali blinked a few times considering it. "Yes, I like the work we're doing. We're making a difference and I'm proud of that." She smiled. "To answer your first question, I'm very excited about marrying Jake and becoming a mother to Heather, although the mother part worries me." She looked at Sara. "I don't know how you do it, Sara, with three kids. How can you let them walk out the door with all the dangers that are out there? A fourteen-year-old boy from Brooklyn died eating candy a couple days ago. Candy! They reported last night that his gummy bears were laced with fentanyl. That's unfathomable to me!"

They walked over to the bed and sat down.

"You're sounding like a mom already, Mali. Every day will be filled with immense joy, an intense love, and a certain level of fear. The best we can do is teach our kids right from wrong, help them understand the good and evil that exists out there, and make sure they know how much they're loved. Those are the building blocks of a good foundation that will prepare them to face the world as adults. It's not easy at times. I wish I could wrap my kids in bubble wrap so they never get hurt and are always safe, but that's not realistic." She reached over and patted Mali's arm. "You're going to be a great mom. Don't forget that you can call me anytime you have questions."

Mali sighed. "I appreciate that and you know I will. I recognize how blessed I am. To say I'm happy is a huge understatement."

They hugged.

"Okay, let me get out of here so you can freshen up. I'll be downstairs in fifteen minutes." Mali rose from the bed and walked to the door. She paused before walking out, and looked over her shoulder at Sara. "Thanks for everything, Sara. I'm glad you're here." She left, closing the door softly behind her.

The rest of the day was a flurry of activity as the group marched from appointment to appointment. Willow was like a drill sergeant ordering the troops here and there in an effort to complete all tasks in the short timeframe allotted. Final alterations to the dresses were made and the rose bouquets and arrangements were designed.

The group stopped at the Philadelphia Country Club, of which Willow and Charles Hooper were long-standing members, for lunch. In keeping with the expectations of their clientele, the restaurant was fine dining at its best with crisp, white linen tablecloths, crystal glasses, and only the best china. Following Willow like ducklings behind its mama, they wove around various tables with Willow waving to some friends. She occasionally stopped to say hello to others and introduce them to her daughter and the rest of the party.

Willow sighed as she sank into her chair. "I took the liberty of ordering for all of us before we arrived, a simple salad for now. We still have to go to the baker for the cake tasting and meet with the photographer. Dinner will be much more substantial." Mali watched her peruse the room and admire the natural light from the floor-to-ceiling windows that covered the back wall. "I do wish you had agreed to have your wedding here, Jasmine."

"Mother, I—"

Willow waved a delicate hand. "Water under the bridge. I know you wanted a more intimate setting."

"I love your gardens, Mother, and couldn't imagine a better setting for my wedding, regardless of the season."

Willow smiled. "Well…" She cleared her throat then looked down at her to-do list. "You still need to give me the music for the string quartet. I have to provide it to them before Christmas so they can prepare."

"That's easy. Any music from the *Nutcracker*, it IS the Christmas season after all, and Vivaldi's *Four Seasons*. You, and everyone in the wedding party before me, will walk in to Pachelbel's 'Canon in D', Father and I will enter with the traditional 'Here Comes the Bride,' and Jake and I will leave to the 'Wedding March.' Anything else?"

Willow opened her mouth to respond but closed it with a wry smile and a shake of her head as their salads were served.

* * *

Mali was sitting on the window seat of the bay window in her bedroom later that evening when the FaceTime call from Jake came in.

"Hey gorgeous, how was your day?"

With a big smile, Mali said, "Non-stop! But we accomplished everything we set out to do."

"Good! It sounds like everything is ready. Did the gals–"

Heather, Jake's daughter, appeared on the screen, interrupting them. "Daddy, I want to say hello."

"It's not polite to interrupt, young lady. What is the proper way to enter a conversation?"

Heather sighed dramatically. "Wait until one person finishes talking then say 'excuse me' before continuing."

"That's right."

Mali smiled at the interaction. At seven years old, Heather was a delightful combination of tomboy and princess, and quite precocious. She always wore pink, her long black hair was either in a ponytail or a braid that her Papa fixed for her every day, and while she preferred to wear jeans, she willingly wore dresses on special occasions, like when the two of them proposed to her. Heather was a bright, funny, and happy child. Mali adored her.

"Well, since you've stopped talking...excuse me, daddy, but I want to say hello." She faced the screen and smiled mischievously at Mali. Jake just shook his head and chuckled. Mali's breath caught in her throat as she looked at the two of them staring at her. Heather was the spitting image of her dad. *I am so fortunate to have these two in my life!*

"Hello sweetheart. Did you have a good day?"

"Hi soon-to-be-mommy. I had a great day with Papa. School was cancelled because of snow. Papa took me to the park instead and we were the only ones there. I slid down the slide even though it had snow on it. I didn't go fast and my butt got super wet." She giggled. "Then Papa pushed me on the swing. I went really high. After that, we built a snowman then came home and we drank hot cocoa with marshmallows in front of the fire. It was yummy." She spoke a mile a minute in her excitement.

Mali laughed. "That was quite a day!"

"Daddy says you're at Grammy and Papa Two's house to finish getting things ready for the wedding." As soon as their engagement was official, Heather had started calling Mali her soon-to-be-mommy and her parents Grammy and Papa Two, which had melted all their hearts. Heather had a way of sneaking inside one's heart without even trying.

"That's right. We finished all of the details and guess what I'm bringing home with me?"

Heather's eyes got round as she bounced up and down, waiting.

"I'm bringing your special dress for the wedding with me. You're going to love it. It's perfect for my flower girl." She smiled as she watched Heather beam with pride. "Grammy told me to tell you that a hair dresser is coming to the house on the morning of the wedding and he's going to fix your hair just like he's going to fix mine."

"So we'll be twins?" Heather's voice rose as she said each word.

"Well, not exactly since your hair is much longer than mine. But it'll be close."

"Yippee!" She jumped up and down. "I've got to go tell Papa the news." With a wave, she ran out of the room calling for her Papa all the way.

Mali and Jake shared a laugh.

"Heather is one special little girl."

"And she loves you very much, Mali, as do I. What time are you heading back tomorrow?"

"We're having breakfast at eight thirty and should be on the road by ten. I'll call you when we get home."

Jake nodded. "Have a good rest and I'll talk to you tomorrow. I love you."

"I love you too."

CHAPTER THREE

Jake's home, Weehawken, NJ
Saturday, December 25, 7:50 a.m.

"What took you so long to get here, soon-to-be-mommy? I've been waiting forever to open presents," exclaimed Heather as she threw open the door when she noticed Mali walking up the steps. She had been peeking through the curtains of the front window waiting for her to arrive.

"Now, Heather," started Jerry, Jake's dad, as he took the packages in Mali's hands and kissed her on the cheek. "Hello Mali. I'd say the wait was worth it, wouldn't you, poppet?"

Laughing, Heather launched herself into Mali's arms. "Absolutely!" Placing her hands on Mali's cheeks, she leaned in close. They were nose to nose. "Merry Christmas!" She smacked her a kiss then leaned back in her arms.

"Merry Christmas, sweetheart. And I arrived as soon as I could. It wasn't easy with all of those packages Papa is putting under that beautiful tree." Standing more than seven feet tall, the tree was covered with strands of popcorn and homemade ornaments. Paper snowflakes, popsicle stick Santas and reindeer, and shiny stars and angels twinkled from the colorful lights that were woven throughout the tree. A white angel made of feathers had the honor of sitting on top.

Heather looked over her shoulder at the tree. "The angel on top is mommy watching over us." Wiggling out of Mali's arms, she skipped over to the tree to help her Papa, shaking each gift before placing them carefully under the tree.

Two strong arms wrapped around Mali's waist from behind. "Merry Christmas, darling," murmured Jake as he pulled her close and nuzzled her neck.

"Hmmmm…Merry Christmas to you." She tipped her head to the side for easier access, shivering as goosebumps covered her arms. "Just one more week," she whispered.

Jake squeezed her tight. "I can't wait," he whispered back.

"A-hem."

Mali and Jake glanced at Jerry and Heather, and burst out laughing. Both were standing with their legs apart, arms crossed, wearing identical expressions of hope and impatience.

"Well, what are you waiting for?" teased Jake as they sauntered over to the sofa and sat down.

Without further ado, Heather tore into her gifts. Wrapping paper flew every which way and cries of delight echoed in the room after each treasure was opened. She made a point of hugging the giver after revealing then exclaiming over each gift before moving on to the next.

The adults opened their gifts with equal delight, if not the same abandon. When all was said and done, the floor couldn't be seen under the paper and boxes, and Heather was sitting in front of the fire introducing her newest doll to the one in the crib next to her.

Mali leaned against Jake as she took everything in.

"Happy?"

"Indescribably." She sighed. "Christmas growing up was nothing like this."

"You didn't celebrate with your parents?"

"We did, but it was…" She paused, thinking. "… civilized, for lack of a better word. All of us sat on chairs or the sofa and Betsy, Mother's maid, handed out each gift. They were opened one at a time and the trash was handed to Roger."

"The butler?"

"Yes. Not one spec of colorful paper ever touched the floor."

"Hmmm…"

"Don't get me wrong. I was appreciative of the gifts I received and we always enjoyed a delicious meal. It was the one time of the year that Mother allowed us to eat in the living room, in front of the tree, instead of at the dining table. But there was no fun or laughter like here." She sighed again. "I'm overwhelmed knowing that this will be my life forever in one week."

Jake leaned down and kissed her. "Forever."

Jerry disappeared into the kitchen, returning with a trash bag.

"Let us help you, Jerry." She nudged Jake up then took

the bag from Jerry. She held it open as the men picked up the wrapping paper and squished each into balls, tossing them into the bag pretending to shoot hoops. The boxes were torn down and placed in the bag as well.

Christmas dinner was a joyous occasion as everyone pitched in to help prepare the side dishes that accompanied the turkey Jerry had placed in the oven earlier. Mashed potatoes with gravy, cornbread stuffing, caesar salad, green bean casserole, and beets, Heather's favorite, adorned the table as Jerry began carving and serving the turkey.

As they ate, conversation turned to the wedding and Mali's family.

"I'm sorry your parents weren't able to come to dinner," said Jerry. "I understand from Jake that you usually have Christmas dinner with your family. I hope they weren't upset that you're here."

"Not at all. They understand, and they appreciated your invitation. But my sisters and their families are with my parents for a couple of days. Mother said it was the perfect time for the final fitting of my sisters' dresses.

"Are your honeymoon plans all set?"

Jake nodded. "We fly to Cabo after the reception. We'll be there for six nights, returning on Friday. The office will be closed from the twenty ninth until January tenth. We'll have the weekend after we return to get settled and to prepare for the work week."

Mali's eyes gleamed. "I've never been to Cabo San Lucas and am looking forward to some sun, sand, and warmth."

Heather finished her dinner and asked to go play with her new toys.

After she left the table, Jerry studied Mali. "Are you sure you don't mind me living here now that you'll be moving in. I know I'm in the casita over the garage but a newly married couple should have their privacy as they start their new life together."

Mali reached over and squeezed Jerry's hand, locking eyes with him. "Of course I don't mind. And I'd be insulted if you left. You're part of my new family and I couldn't imagine this place without you."

Jerry swallowed hard, blinked fast a few times, and nodded.

"Besides," Jake added, "who's going to take care of Heather when we're working?" He winked at his dad.

"Son…" Jerry smiled and shook his head.

"It's settled then." Mali stood and picked up some plates. "You two go and play with Heather while I clean up."

"I'll help." Jake reached over to pick up the mashed potatoes and rolls.

"No, I'm taking care of things today. Scoot, both of you. I'll bring out the pumpkin pie and ice cream shortly." She pushed the swinging door open with her hip and disappeared inside the kitchen.

* * *

Home of Jeremiah Ashton, Denver
Tuesday, December 28, 4:15 p.m.

Eight nine-year-olds were racing around the back yard, playing tag and jumping in the yellow, green, and red jumpy house that had been rented. It was Jeremiah

Ashton's birthday and his party was in full swing. It was a sunny day, albeit a little chilly at fifty degrees. The kids didn't notice or didn't care. They were screaming and laughing, and having the best of times.

Most of the fathers were outside watching the kids. Jeremiah's dad was preparing the coals for the barbecue. His mom, Lorraine, and the remaining adults, were inside drinking wine and chatting as Lorraine made the burger patties and placed them, along with the hot dogs, on a platter ready for the grill. The other moms worked on the side dishes, and Lorraine's sister was decorating the cake.

Jeremiah threw open the door and raced inside with two of his buddies, pushing a few chairs out of the way and running between the sofa and coffee table. They were headed for the stairs.

"Hold it right there, birthday boy. Where are you going?"

Jeremiah screeched to a stop, his friends bumping into him as they, too, stopped. He looked at his mom, a hopeful smile on his face. "I want to show Bobby and Dean my new app game."

Lorraine was shaking her head before Jeremiah even finished talking. "You have guests outside. Go." She pointed her finger to the door.

"Aw, mom." With shoulders slumped and head down, Jeremiah trudged to the back door. "Come on guys. I'll have to show it to you another time." As he opened the door, he perked up. "Last one to the fort is a rotten egg!" He shot out of the door, his friends right behind him.

Lorraine laughed as she returned to her preparations.

Even as she listened to her friends talking, she thought about how lucky she was to have had Jeremiah. She and Tom had been married for eighteen years. The first three years of their marriage were spent getting their finances in order and buying a house. They had tried for five years after that to have a child and had almost given up when, miracle of miracles, she had discovered she was pregnant. He was their only child and they adored him. Every day was a joy. She sighed, finding it hard to believe he was already nine years old. *Time goes by in a flash.* She picked up the platter and carried it outside to her husband.

Twenty-five minutes later, all of the boys were sitting at the table inside munching on hamburgers and hot dogs, a variety of chips, and potato salad, leaving the coleslaw, vegetable tray, and fruit salad to the adults. They were talking nonstop, one on top of the other. Lorraine chuckled as she watched them. She had no idea how they understood what was being said, it was all jumbled together. But they seemed to know. It was loud and boisterous, and full of giggles. Lorraine smiled at her husband over the heads of the children.

After the paper plates were tossed and the table cleared, the cake was brought in and a chorus of Happy Birthday rang in the room. Jeremiah blew out the candles and each boy received a large piece. They dug into the three-layer Neapolitan cake, each exclaiming over the particular flavor they enjoyed the best, whether vanilla, chocolate, or strawberry.

As the parents sat down for coffee, Jeremiah sidled up to his mom. "Can I give my friends their candy bags?"

"Normally, the treats are given as guests are leaving but, yes, go ahead and give it to them. Why don't you all go upstairs? Dad can put on *Sandlot* for you."

"Really? I love that movie! Thanks Mom!"

He kissed her on the cheek then ran over to his dad, evidently asking him to put the movie on upstairs.

Lorraine watched as Tom excused himself and headed upstairs with the boys following, each holding their treats bag that Jeremiah had just given them and hopping up each stair in their excitement.

The adults enjoyed a lively conversation while drinking coffee, occasionally commenting on the fun day the boys were having and the cheering they heard upstairs.

Around seven-thirty, Lorraine stood up. "I haven't heard anything upstairs for awhile except for the movie. That can only mean trouble where eight boys are concerned." Everyone laughed, knowing the trouble that boys can get into. "I'm going to check on them." She left the group, walking up the stairs and out of sight.

A moment later, the adults heard a blood-curdling scream. Tom jumped up and raced upstairs, closely followed by the rest of the men and women. They all slowed to a stop in confusion as they entered the playroom and took in the scene. Two of the boys were unconscious, four were lying on their sides vomiting non-stop. One boy was sitting on a chair, weaving side to side and moaning.

Lorraine was crouched in front of Jeremiah, who was leaning back on the couch. He looked sleepy, out of it, and was mumbling about being dizzy and not feeling well. Crying hysterically, Lorraine implored, "Tom,

Tom, oh my God, what's wrong with them?" She shook Jeremiah. His head rolled to the side and his glassy, unseeing eyes stared down at nothing. "Jeremiah, honey, wake up. Tell mommy what's wrong."

All parents ran to their children, the mothers screaming and crying, the dads trying to hold it together as they reached their children, none understanding what was happening.

Lorraine didn't notice when Tom called the police nor when he rejoined her after the call. She had climbed up onto the couch and pulled Jeremiah into her arms. She rocked back and forth, holding her son, knowing he was dead, wailing, the pain unbearable.

The deaths of the eight boys made national news. Fentanyl-laced lollipops were the culprits. They were each found to contain more than three milligrams of fentanyl. Two milligrams, the equivalent of four grains of salt, can kill an average adult. The boys didn't stand a chance. Lorraine had told the police that she bought the candy online at a site she had used before. The DEA officially took over the investigation.

CHAPTER FOUR

The Hooper House, Philadelphia
Saturday, January 1, 7:15 a.m.

"GOING TO THE chapel and you're gonna get ma-a-a-ried," a chorus of the old tune rang in Mali's ears as Beth, Kirsten, Jen, and Heather danced into her room to wake her up. Mali rolled onto her back with a sleepy grin, wiping the sleep out of her eyes as they continued singing and dancing all over the room, ending at her bed.

"Good morning, soon-to-be-mommy!" exclaimed Heather as she climbed on the end of the bed then bounced her way up to Mali, landing on her stomach.

"Ooof!" Mali tried to breathe and laugh at the same time, her hands automatically reaching up to grasp Heather by the waist. She ended up coughing, with Heather shaking each time Mali coughed, sending her into a fit of giggles.

"Good morning to you, sweetheart," returned Mali when she could speak. She pulled her down for a kiss, turning her head to acknowledge her friends. "Hi guys! Thanks for that warm awakening at…what time is it?"

She glanced at the clock on the nightstand and groaned. "Seven-fifteen? You woke me up at seven-fifteen?"

"You bet we did," Kirsten hooted. "Just like you did to me back at Quantico during training when I forgot to set my alarm. Of course, you sang the "Star Spangled Banner" and it was four-forty-five. Consider yourself lucky we waited until now."

Mali stuck her tongue out at Kirsten as everyone laughed. Moving Heather to the side, she sat up and looked around. Her serene room was anything but that ever since she arrived two days ago. Her wedding dress was hanging on the door of the closet, Heather's dress right next to it. Her bright red suitcase, spread out on top of the cushions at the bay window, was partially filled with clothes for her honeymoon. The top of the dresser had various bottles of perfume and other sundries one evidently needed for a wedding, as well as a large vase of red roses, and the bathroom counter was covered with makeup and other toiletries.

The stunning two-piece white dress she wore for the rehearsal dinner and party last night was lying on the floor in a heap, exactly where she had stepped out of it. Mali's insides melted again as she remembered the look on Jake's face when he first watched her walk downstairs. The flirty crop sweetheart bodice was covered in intricate floral lace, trimmed with scalloped details and short cap sleeves, and the skirt, made of lightweight chiffon, floated to the floor from a high waist and finished with a side slit up to mid-thigh. Jake had said she was a vision and couldn't take his eyes off her.

"I've never seen your space, whether here or at home in the City, in such a state," observed Sara as she looked around. She gasped. "Your beautiful dress! How could you leave it on the floor," she chided as she rushed over and picked it up then laid it over the back of a chair next to the window.

"I was so sleepy last night," she mumbled.

Jen stared at her with narrowed eyes. "Well, it doesn't look like you got much sleep. We're going to have our work cut out for us this morning," she teased.

Mali stuck her tongue out again, this time at Jen, then threw the covers aside and stood up.

Her wedding day. She was getting married today. She bit her lip to contain the scream that threatened to escape. She practically pranced to the window to look down into the gardens, clasping her hands to her chest as she gazed outside. Heather ran over to stand on the cushions next to the suitcase, and her friends joined her to take in the spectacle.

There was a flurry of activity as workers finished preparing the area for the ceremony. Any snow where the wedding would be held had long been removed the night before. A large white tent was erected in the gardens beyond the pool and Mali noticed a few chairs inside, through the opening that she and her father would walk through. What captured her attention, however, were the dozens and dozens of roses everywhere. Large urns of red roses lined both sides of the red carpet that had been rolled out from the back patio to the tent entrance, disappearing inside. Workers carried smaller urns into the tent while others took portable heaters inside. Two large baskets of rose pedals were sitting next to the pool ready to be tossed onto its surface right before the guests arrived.

The morning looked crisp but it was crystal clear. The snow on the bushes and trees outside the tent area and around the pool began to sparkle as the sun's rays touched upon each of them one by one. Looking up, Mali was sure that she had never seen such a vivid blue sky. She was mesmerized.

"It's beautiful!" exclaimed Heather. "Can I run down and smell the roses?"

Mali touched Heather's cheek with her finger. "Why don't you wake up Daddy and Papa, although I suspect they're already up, and go down with one of them." Heather had not seen her father since last night, opting to sleep with Beth instead.

"Ooooh!" She jumped off her perch and skipped to the door. Throwing it open, they could hear the patter of her slippers as she raced down the hall, calling for her daddy the entire way.

Beth chuckled as she closed the door. "Heather is such a sweet girl. I wanted to tell you that last night, after I said goodnight to her and went into the bathroom, I heard her talking. I cracked open the door to see what she was doing and almost started crying." She walked over to Mali as she was talking. "She was praying and telling God to make sure that her mommy knew how much she loved her and would never forget her even though she was going to have a new mommy that she loved very much starting tomorrow. And she said she was happy that her daddy was happy and thanked God for bringing you to them."

"Awwww..." Kirsten and Jen sighed.

Mali put her hand on her chest, tearing up. "How–" She blinked a few times and cleared her throat. "I keep saying this, but how did I get so lucky?"

"You deserve it!" said Beth with a smile. "Group hug everyone!"

The four friends hugged each other then started to sing. "Going to the chapel...", laughing and dancing all over the room. They abruptly stopped and turned toward the door when they heard a knock.

Willow breezed in with Roger, who pushed a cart filled with croissants, jam, an array of fruits, orange juice, and coffee for the bride and her bridesmaids. "Good morning, ladies." She glided to Mali, took her hands, and leaned in to kiss her on each cheek. "I'd ask how you're doing but I heard the laughter and singing all the way down the hall." She smiled. "Are you ready for today?"

Mali nodded and squeezed her mother's hands. "And for the rest of my life. Thank you for everything, Mother. It looks beautiful outside, like a fairy tale."

Willow sniffed. "Only the best for my daughter."

"This breakfast looks great! Thanks Mrs. H," said Kirsten, not comfortable calling her Willow. "I'm starving!"

Willow smiled. "I'll leave you to it for now." She headed to the door. "Henri will be here with his team at precisely nine o'clock to prepare your hair and makeup. Jana will arrive at nine-thirty and will start taking pictures outside while the videographer sets up. I've already told Jake and Jerry to be ready for her at nine-forty-five. Heather will join her father and grandfather for pictures, please make sure she's ready. You'll follow at ten-fifteen, although I'm sure she'll pop in to get some pictures as you're dressing. Guests will start arriving at ten-thirty and the ceremony will begin precisely at eleven. I asked the string quartet to arrive at eight thirty so we can enjoy music throughout the morning."

"Mother…" Mali paused. Willow stopped and turned back. "You'll be here as I'm getting ready, right? I'd like some pictures of the two of us and also some with Heather."

Willow's face softened as she studied her daughter. "Of course I'll be here." With that, she turned and left, closing the door behind her.

"She is not how you have described her, Mali," said Beth. "When you asked her to be here for pictures with you, I thought she was going to cry."

Mali was still staring at the closed door. She took a deep breath then smiled at her friends. "She's changed, as has my father, ever since the hunted game. I never knew I could have this kind of relationship with either of them." She sighed.

"This croissant is melting in my mouth," stated Kirsten, her mouth stuffed full.

Everyone laughed but when Jen snorted, which rarely if ever happened, they all roared. The humor and laughter continued throughout the morning as they finished their light meal and prepared for the wedding.

10:45 a.m.

Mali stood in front of the mirror as her mother wove the delicate crown of baby's breath and miniature red roses into her hair while Jana took pictures. At the back of the crown was a French Alencon lace veil that hung to her waist in the back.

"There." Willow looked pleased. Hands on Mali's shoulders, she gazed at her in the mirror. "Beautiful!" Mali was stunning. Her off-the-shoulder fitted bodice with its sweetheart neckline was covered in lace that matched her veil. Embroidered appliqués carried through the long sleeves and cascaded down the Tulle ball gown skirt. The scalloped hemline completed the look.

Mali beamed.

"Hold that look," stated Jana as she circled them while snapping pictures. "Okay, where's Heather? Let's get some pictures with the three of you in front of the mirror."

Heather, who was standing next to Beth, Kirsten, and Jen, skipped over to Mali, all smiles. "We look like twins," she exclaimed. Her dress had a lace overlay similar to Mali's. The contrast between the simple crown of baby's breath on her head and her jet black hair, now in single French braid that hung down her back, was stunning. With the exception of her hair, they could have been mother and daughter.

Mali touched Heather's cheek. "You look lovely, Heather."

More pictures were taken but all eyes turned to the door when, after a sharp knock, Charles opened it and strode inside. His step faltered when he took in the scene. His mouth moved but no words came out. He shook his head and cleared his throat. When he spoke, his voice was gruff, filled with emotion. "You are lovely, Jasmine. You remind me of your mother on our wedding day." He gazed at Willow, and an emotion that looked like love, in Mali's opinion, passed between them.

"Thank you, Father."

He clapped his hands. "It's time for a wedding. Shall we go?"

Excited giggles and laughter echoed in the hall as everyone made their way to the stairs, Mali holding on to her father's arm. He stopped at the top of the stairs as Jana hustled down to take pictures. Willow led the procession down. When they reached the entrance to the porch, Jerry stepped forward and smiled at Willow, offering her his arm.

The soft sounds of "Canon in D" signaled the start of the ceremony as Willow and Jerry began the long walk down the red carpet to the tent and inside. Heather followed with her basket of rose pedals, giggling and dancing her way to the altar. The guests chuckled as she passed them, tossing the petals with a flourish. Jake beamed with pride. Jen and Kirsten each followed with Joe Alters and Felix Johnson, two of their coworkers on the task force. Sara, as the maid of honor, was the last to walk down the aisle with Jeff Cink, the best man and Jake's Army buddy, who also served as a consultant on the task force.

As soon as Sara and Jeff entered the tent, Charles paused, studying his daughter. "I'm very proud of you, Jasmine, and not just because you're getting married today." He smiled at the look on her face. "Ready?"

At her nod, they stepped off the porch. With each step, her heart began to race. She bit her lip, sure her heart was going to burst out of her chest, it was filled with love. As they neared the tent and "Here Comes the Bride" began, her father slowed his step and patted her hand that was resting on his arm, smiling down at her. She glanced at their hands, only then noticing the death grip she had on his arm. Remembering whose daughter she was, she inhaled deeply before slowly releasing her breath and relaxing her shoulders and grip. Holding her head high, she nodded slightly and they stepped inside.

Everyone stood but they were just a blur of color. She only had eyes for Jake. He was so handsome, standing tall in his black tuxedo, crisp white shirt and deep red cummerbund. He took her breath away.

The ceremony was simple and heartfelt. *The Herald* later reported that there wasn't a dry eye in the tent when they observed Jake wiping a tear from Mali's eye before leaning down to kiss his bride. The reception was described as intimate and lavish, with champagne flowing freely. The gracious bride glided from guest to guest to make sure everyone was enjoying themselves. There was laughter, cheers, and non-stop dancing. More tears were shed when Jake picked up Heather, as they stood ready to leave for their honeymoon, and the new family squeezed tight in a hug.

"This hug has to last all week!" Those near enough to hear Heather speak those words laughed through more tears.

The marriage of Jacob Black and Jasmine Hooper was proclaimed the social event of the year.

For Mali, it was the beginning of the rest of her life.

CHAPTER FIVE

Grand Solmar Lands End Resort & Spa
Penthouse Suite
Cabo San Lucas, Mexico
Tuesday, January 4, 7:10 a.m.

"WAKE UP, SLEEPYHEAD." Jake nuzzled Mali's shoulder as he pulled her closer, spoon fashion.

Mali shook her head. "Hmmmm…just a few more minutes of sleep." Her words belied her actions, though, when she pulled his arm over her back so that it just happened to fall on her breast as she wiggled her bottom suggestively.

"You are naughty, Mrs. Black." His voice deepened with his growing passion. "Maybe you're right. It's too early. But I'm not sleepy." He nipped her ear, causing her to shiver. In one smooth move, he rolled her onto her back and beneath him. He was now lying on top of her. She spread her legs and wrapped them around his waist as he cupped her face with his hands. Staring at each other, he leaned down and kissed her, sliding into her at the same time. Both groaned.

When Mali's eyes slid closed, Jake whispered, "Don't."

"I'm dizzy," Mali whispered back.

Jake pulled back and waited at her entrance, arms shaking as he held himself above her.

Mali opened her eyes. "Don't stop," she panted. Her hands at his waist squeezed and released, squeezed and released.

His eyes captured hers. "I want you to watch what I'm doing to you."

Mali swallowed and licked her lips. Moving one hand down to his manhood, she stroked him once, twice. "Two can play this game, Mr. Black," she teased, her voice thick with passion.

Eyes darkening, he grabbed her wrists and held them above her head as he rammed inside her then pulled almost completely out. Both gasped. He repeated it, moving slowly, with intent. She matched him, urging him to go faster but he kept the pace slow. When she slid her feet down over his buttocks to the back of his thighs, he growled. They continued this dance of love until, releasing her hands, he grabbed her and rolled onto his back giving her control. Immediately, Mali pushed herself into a sitting position and, hands on his chest, rode him faster and faster. His hands and words urged her on. Panting, moaning, she edged over the precipice, screaming his name, and taking him with her.

When awareness returned, Mali sat up and stared at Jake beneath her. Eyes still closed, he smiled and rested his hands on her hips. Somberly, she ran her fingers over four scars, thinking of the pain he must have endured. A lone tear tracked down her cheek.

Opening his eyes, he wiped away her tear and lifted her chin until her eyes met his. "They don't hurt."

"I know. I just keep imagining those bullets hitting you."

"It was a long time ago."

"I…"

Jake shifted her off his body and rolled to the side, sitting up in one smooth motion. He placed his feet on the floor, his back now to her.

"I'm starving," Jake pronounced, rubbing his stomach.

Mali sighed. He had never told her about his time in special ops while in the Army. He wasn't going to today either.

"If you're not hungry for one thing, you're hungry for another," she teased, to lighten the mood.

He looked over his shoulder. "You got that right!" He grinned, making a move to grab her.

Shrieking, she scrambled out of bed. "No sir. We need sustenance of another kind." She shrugged into a red silk robe and walked to the slider door leading to the large patio of their suite. The only way to access the main part of the penthouse suite from the bedroom was via the private patio. The sounds of the ocean greeted her as she opened the slider and stepped outside. She could hear the waves lapping against the wall below and seagulls cawing above as they searched for food. The slider leading into the main area was made of three ten-foot-tall by four-foot-wide glass doors. It was fully open, the glass doors tucked into the pocket enabling Mali to walk right into the dining room and kitchen. She was making coffee when Jake ambled in, wearing loose black swim trunks.

"I called in our breakfast. It should be here in a few minutes."

Mali smiled.

"I still can't believe Charles upgraded our beautiful room to this penthouse suite. Four bedrooms? Over six thousand square feet? What was he thinking?" He shook his head as he accepted the mug of coffee from Mali.

"That's my father just being my father. He said he wanted to treat us since the wedding was so affordable." She laughed. "He never uses that word." She sipped her coffee then walked over to the other set of slider pocket doors. She slid it open and pushed it into the pocket. The living room was now fully open to the outdoors and their private pool and hot tub. Looking back at Jake, she added, "We have enjoyed each of those bedrooms, multiple times, I might add." With a saucy grin, she dropped her robe and walked over to the pool, her coffee still in her hand. Easing into the refreshing water, she glided to the negative edge and set her coffee on the ledge. Resting her forearms next to the mug, she watched a sailboat float by in the distance. "Ahhhh. I could get used to this."

She heard the doorbell ring and Jake speak with the concierge a moment later, although it didn't register what was being said. Wheels squeaked on the tile flooring and glasses clinked, gradually getting louder.

Turning from the view, Mali watched Jake roll the trolley, filled with food, out onto the patio.

"Breakfast, m'lady," he smiled as he positioned it next to a cushioned lounger, large enough for the two of them.

"Mmmm…smells delicious." She climbed out of the pool, thanked Jake with a kiss when he wrapped her in a towel, then both sat down to eat.

"What would you like to do today?" he asked, as he buttered a piece of toast.

Mali swallowed her bite of ham and cheese omelet. "This is our third day here and we haven't left the suite. I want to check out the resort then go into town."

"Hey, we've been busy." He wiggled his eyebrows up and down.

She threw a piece of bacon at him.

Laughing, he popped it in his mouth. "Your wish is my command. Let's go after we eat before it gets too hot. I'll arrange for a car to drive us to town and we'll explore the area."

Mali nodded.

They finished their meal, showered, then walked downstairs and out back, winding their way through tables and loungers, and past the resort's outdoor bar and massive infinity pool. Mali deliberately took a longer route to get to the lobby. She wanted to explore more of the resort. When they arrived a few days ago, she had only seen glimpses of it as they were escorted to their suite.

As they meandered along, she exclaimed over the palm trees that waved in the breeze, the colorful flowers, and the sound of the ocean as the waves hit the beach. She stopped to smell some flowers before she marveled at the rock outcropping the resort backed up against. Some elements were even incorporated into the design of the hotel.

Lands End was fitting for the name of the resort. Located at the southernmost tip of Baja, the city of Cabo San Lucas and the bay was on one side and the open ocean was on the other. Mali slipped off her sandals and stepped onto the beach. She giggled as the sand squished through her toes and tickled her feet. By mutual consent, they approached the water's edge and stopped to enjoy the view. Waves gently folded over the sand and their feet. They watched two jet skis race across the water, the laughter of the occupants reaching their ears. Further down the beach, three seagulls vied for food that a young boy was holding up. Their chatter and the boy's giggles made Mali smile.

"This is beautiful, so peaceful."

"Yes it is."

When Mali glanced at Jake, she noticed that he was staring at her. Blushing, she smiled her thanks then tugged on his hand. "Come on."

They returned to the pool area where a few children were splashing on one end, while their parents sat on loungers nearby. Many loungers were empty of people but had towels, paperback novels, suntan lotion, and other items scattered across them to hold them for later. A group of young adults were taking pictures nearby, and others were gathered at the bar. *I guess it's five o'clock somewhere*, she mused. Mariachi music was playing and the smell of hamburgers filled the air.

Mali and Jake began to cross a bridge that arched over the pool splitting it in half, and stopped in the middle to take in their surroundings.

"This resort is lovely. I'm glad we came here, Jake. Let's take a picture to send to Heather and your dad."

He pulled out his phone to take a selfie. As they snuggled to get the best shot with the ocean behind them, Jake snapped the picture then they continued on to the lobby.

Neither noticed the gringo leaning against a palm tree on the other side of the pool, who was staring at Jake as though he had seen a ghost.

* * *

"Teniente. It's him, I'm sure of it."

"No es posible, Cenzo. That pendejo was killed six years ago after he murdered el jefe grande. I was there."

"So was I. Mira, I took a picture. Sending ahora." He clicked the send button on his phone.

"Dios mio. When did you take this?"

"Ten minutes ago at the Grand Solmar. He's with a woman." He paused. "What should I do, teniente? And what about Salazar?"

Silence.

"Teniente?"

"Forget about Salazar for now. Necesito hablar con el jefe. Find out everything you can about him and call me in one hour." The line went dead.

Matt Spencer placed his phone in his pocket and rubbed the back of his neck. His thoughts turned inward as he remembered the day he fled the United States for greener pastures, not realizing he would meet his true family.

He left San Diego ten years ago, disillusioned after his divorce. To say he was surprised when he was served with divorce papers was an understatement. Their romance hit them both hard and fast. She had the dark, sultry looks that men drooled over, and with his blond hair and blue-eyed beach boy looks, they made a striking couple. Everyone had said so. They were married two months after their first date, eloping to Las Vegas. She was a legal assistant at a law office in Carlsbad; she had never asked him what he did or where he got his money. But she certainly enjoyed spending it, he remembered with a bitter taste in his mouth. So he enjoyed the occasional snort and sold crack and meth to make money. He did it for her and all she did was nag, nag, nag. She was completely unreasonable and, upon reflection, he was actually glad that she had kicked him out. He was better off without her. Deciding to go where the action was, he had turned south.

Joining the Los Rinches cartel was the best thing that had ever happened to him. He still laughed when he reflected on the cartel's name. In English, it's a pejorative term for the border patrol. He loved the irony and felt that he couldn't have picked a better cartel to join.

It had taken awhile to prove himself and to be trusted. They made him do crazy things to prove he was worthy. His first beheading was the most difficult. Immediately afterward, he had shaken himself like a bird shakes its feathers after a rain and promptly puked his guts out, much to the amusement of those who were "training" him. It got easier over time, and he now approached each task with enthusiasm.

His proudest moment was the day they had named him *Cenzo*. They had likened him to the cenzontle, or northern mockingbird, with his diminutive stature, the way he shook himself after each kill, and his ability to accurately copy the sound of any animal and, more importantly, any person. That was the day Matt Spencer had ceased to exist.

His special abilities had been used on more than one occasion to the benefit of the cartel, rocketing him to a position of prominence that he relished.

Salazar was an up-and-coming globalist with money, who could possibly be an asset to their organization. Cenzo was sent to Cabo to determine if he could be a friend, or would be a foe. Seeing the major walking over the bridge was purely coincidental.

The major had been part of a group of U.S. soldiers who had infiltrated the cartel that fateful night six years ago, killing their jefe grande and numerous others. Jefe's wife and son had escaped but his two daughters were also killed. The hell that had been unleashed was one he would never forget. He barely made it out of there alive, along with the teniente and two others. The rest of the soldiers were slaughtered. How was it possible that the major was still alive? Before escaping, he watched as the major fell, multiple bullets hitting him.

Jefe's son, despite being only sixteen at the time, had

stepped into his father's role, changing the cartel over time into something more vicious and feared, and much more powerful. He shifted the business from cocaine to fentanyl and was working with the Chinese to distribute it in the United States. He had also set up a massive lab and distribution center inside the U.S. to expedite deliveries. That fateful day, el nuevo jefe had vowed to take down those who killed his father and sisters.

Shaking thoughts of the past from his mind, he straightened up and strode to the lobby. He had work to do.

Walking inside, he approached the reception counter. Three women were talking to each other behind the counter. No guests were near the reception area so one of the women walked to the side and smiled as he approached.

"Hola amor." Cenzo picked up her delicate hand and kissed her palm, giving her his sexiest smile.

She blushed. "Hola Cenzo. How are you today?"

"Better, now that I am near you." Cenzo was pouring on the charm, not only to get the information he desired but also because he wanted her in his bed. If he was truthful, the charm was more for the latter than the former. But it would serve both.

She giggled.

He leaned over the reception counter to whisper in her ear. "I want to take you to dinner tonight." He made it sound like something other than food would be on the menu. "What time do you get off work?" He pulled back to look into her face.

Her brown eyes darkened as she leaned toward him and stared into his eyes. "I get off at three." Her breath caught in her throat as she peeked at his mouth.

Looking down at her ripe breasts practically bursting out of her crisp, white work shirt, he felt himself grow hard. "I look forward to..." He licked his lips. "... eating with you." He leaned a little closer, his mouth almost touching hers. "I need a little information first, if that's all right, amor."

She swayed back, breathing hard. "What kind of information?"

"I'm pretty sure I recognized an old associate of mine from the United States, someone I haven't seen in years. He's here with a woman."

"I'm not supposed to give out information on guests. Besides, there are a lot of couples here, Cenzo."

"I understand, but I'm hoping you can make an exception. If you saw them, you wouldn't be able to forget them. He's tall with dark hair. Some would consider him good looking, although not nearly as good looking as me." He winked at her. Her giggle was the reaction he had hoped for. "She has red hair, also tall, gorgeous."

Anna nodded. "Ah, you mean Jacob and Mali Black. They're here on their honeymoon, arrived two or three days ago. They passed through the lobby a few minutes ago. You just missed them."

"So it is Jacob. I didn't know he got married. Is he still with Jay's Consulting?"

Anna shrugged.

"Amor," he leaned toward her again. "I need more

information about Jacob. Can you get it for me? I'll make it worth your while, starting with our afternoon and evening together." He briefly touched his lips to hers.

She bit her lip and glanced at the two women at the other end of the counter, who were now reviewing a document. "I'll…I'll try. What do you want to know?"

After telling her some of the things he needed to know, he whispered, "Amor, I can't wait until three to kiss you. Bring any information you can gather to me at the restrooms in ten minutes. I want to show you what you mean to me and what we have to look forward to this afternoon."

Blushing, she nodded. "There's an alcove just past the women's restroom down the hall. I'll be there in ten." She smiled then turned to one of the monitors.

Cenzo waved to everyone as he sauntered through the lobby then backtracked to the alcove she mentioned. He smiled. They would have plenty of privacy.

It seemed like hours, but it was only minutes when she stepped into the alcove. Cenzo pulled her close and kissed her like he was a starved man. His tongue delved in and out of her mouth, mimicking what he wanted to do with the rest of her. He groaned when she responded in kind. Her hands pulled him closer, groaning when she felt his arousal. Unbuttoning her shirt two buttons, he slipped his hands inside, almost losing it when he felt her ripe breasts and tight nipples. She gasped in his mouth when he squeezed both.

"Cenzo," she pushed away slightly, taking a few deep

breaths. "I need air. And we need to stop before someone sees us."

"I don't care if the whole world watches us. You are beautiful and hot and I want to be inside you." He nibbled his way to her ear. Remembering his first goal, he finally pulled back. They stared at each other, both trying to catch their breath.

Licking her lips and taking a final deep breath, she retreated one step and buttoned the two buttons Cenzo had undone. Smiling, she reached into her pocket and pulled out a piece of paper. Handing it to him, she said, "This is all I could find. I bet he'll be excited when he finds out you're here. If I see him, I'll tell him you're looking for him."

"NO!"

Startled, she gasped, falling back another step.

"I'm sorry, amor. But that would ruin the surprise, no? Can you keep this secret, for me?"

Confused, she said, "Of course. They probably won't be back before I get off today anyway. Mr. Black said they'd be back for dinner."

Cenzo nodded. "Excellent." He leaned down to kiss her once more. "I'll pick you up out front just after three. I can't wait."

"Me too." She leaned forward to kiss him once more, then smoothing her hair, she turned and left.

Cenzo opened the paper she had given him, smiling when he read the information. Teniente would be pleased. A shame about Anna though.

CHAPTER SIX

Tuesday, January 4, 5:00 p.m.

"We need to call your dad and Heather today. They're three hours ahead, and should be finished with dinner, right?"

Jake nodded. "They're probably getting ready to watch a show. Let's do it." He stood up from where they were snuggling on the patio and walked inside, returning a few moments later with his phone.

He dialed the number and waited while it rang. "Hi Dad. We thought we'd check in on you and Heather. We're on speaker, by the way."

"Hey son, Mali. We're doing just fine, about to watch the second or third *Ice Age*. I can never keep track of them." He chuckled. "How is Cabo?"

"It's beautiful," replied Mali. "And warm. We're sitting by the pool right now." She laughed. "That sounds much better than watching the snow fall. How are you, Dad?"

"Great. Sitting here watching the snow fall." Everyone laughed. "I'm glad you're enjoying yourselves.

Hang on a sec. Heather, Daddy and Mommy are on the phone."

Jake squeezed Mali's hand when they heard Jerry call out to Heather and then heard her subsequent excited scream.

"Daddy! Mommy! How are you? Are you swimming a lot? Did you ride on a jet ski like you said you would? Is it pretty there?"

"Whoa pumpkin," laughed Jake. "Mommy and I are great! The water is warm and we've enjoyed the pool and the ocean. We have not ridden on a jet ski yet, we plan to tomorrow. And it's beautiful here. Did I answer everything?"

"What's your favorite part of your honeymoon?"

Jake grinned and winked at Mali. "We toured Cabo San Lucas today and enjoyed the sights. That's my favorite so far."

"My favorite part is lounging by the pool and soaking up some sun. What have you been doing since we left?"

"Papa and I stayed with Grammy and Papa Two for another night after the wedding. They had a big fire in the living room. Auntie Lily played the piano. I sat right next to her. I want to learn how to play, Daddy. Oh, then my new cousins and I played games upstairs until it was time to get ready for bed. Papa and I sang songs almost the entire way home. Then yesterday, Papa's friends came over and I watched *Ice Age* on TV. We're watching it again tonight. It's a different one though. Today, I had to go back to school. When do you come home?" She spoke fast, as usual, the words almost running together in her excitement.

Jake answered. "We'll be home on Friday, in three days."

"That's a long way away. I'm counting the days until you get home. I have to take care of my babies now. Love you. Bye." And she was gone.

Mali laughed. "That girl has a lot to say."

They talked with Jerry for another fifteen minutes before saying their goodbyes.

"Your dad is really amazing, and he adores Heather."

Jake nodded. "He was a godsend after Christa passed away, gave up his regular routine with his buddies to take care of us. Moving in with him was the best thing."

"For him as well. I have no doubt that he willingly gave up his old routine to have the opportunity to spend more time with you and Heather." She squeezed his hand and stood up. "I'm going to take a quick shower then get dressed for dinner and dancing. You promised me a night out tonight and I'm not letting you off the hook." She grinned down at him then walked toward the bathroom. "We can't forget to buy some gifts to take home to them. Let's do that tomorrow. I saw a cute little dress when we were in town earlier that would look adorable on Heather." She disappeared around the corner, still talking about things she wanted to buy.

* * *

Weehawken, NJ
Thursday, January 6, 4:20 p.m.

Jerry opened the door from the garage leading into the kitchen and set down the bags of food he carried. He was leaving on Saturday with two of his buddies on an overnight ice fishing trip after the kids returned from their honeymoon. He'd been running errands since lunch. He was tasked with providing the breakfast items, steak and potatoes. *No bunny food for these ice fishing macho men.* He grinned. Paul and George were bringing beer, snacks, and bait. They were staying in a cabin near their favorite lake. It wasn't frozen over yet so they'd be fishing from the pier outside the cabin but they could care less. They just enjoyed the time together and away from the crowds. They'd been doing this every year now for about fifteen years, as best he could recall.

He didn't have to worry about picking up Heather today. She was going to a friend's house and the girl's mother was picking them both up at school.

Pulling the ribeye steaks, potatoes, eggs, sausage, crescent rolls, and cookies out of the bags, he noticed the blinking light on his answering machine. While he had a cell phone, he was old school and preferred a landline. Jacob was always complaining that he couldn't reach his father at times because he forgot to carry his cell more often than not. Jerry chuckled to himself knowing he'd never change.

Walking to the phone and answering machine, he pressed the play button. His buddy, Paul, had called reminding him to get bacon instead of sausage because the latter gave him gas. *Ooops, too late old friend. Just keep your farts to yourself.* He laughed at that thought. Paul also said he'd be over later to pick up the stuff. Since he was driving tomorrow, he wanted everything in its place on the boat he was pulling, tonight. *Done.* Jerry deleted the message and waited to listen to the second message.

The second call was from Jacob. "Hi Dad. Just wanted to let you know that we sent you a little something from Cabo. It may melt so be sure to open it right away. We hope you and Heather enjoy it. See you tomorrow. Love you, Dad."

Jerry smiled as he opened the refrigerator to put the groceries away. *So thoughtful.*

He was just shoving the plastic bags in the holder when he heard a knock on the door. He pushed through the swinging door and walked past the dining and living rooms to the front door. Opening it, he smiled in delight when he glimpsed a small rectangular box in brown wrapping sitting on the welcome mat. He waved to the delivery driver, who was pulling away from the curb, then leaned down and picked it up. There were some markings on the box that kind of looked Spanish to him. He figured it must be from Jake and Mali. Closing the door, he ambled to the sofa, shaking the box as he sat down. Pulling his pocket knife out of his shirt pocket, he paused. *Should I wait for Heather to get home from her play date?* Shaking his head, he remembered what Jake said and decided to proceed. He wouldn't want anything to melt, after all, and Heather wouldn't be home until seven.

Cutting the seam down the middle of the box, he peeled back the lid and looked inside.

"Nice," he exclaimed as he pulled out four bars of Mexican chocolate. The last time he had enjoyed Mexican chocolate was when he was in Puerto Vallarta with his wife, Gloria, the year before she passed. He looked at the picture of her on the wall and sighed. *That trip was amazing. I'm grateful I took her there. I didn't want to go initially. How stupid of me! Thank God she insisted. How is it possible that she's been gone fourteen years? Seems like yesterday when I said goodbye to the love of my life. How she would have loved the man Jake had become, and she would have adored Heather.*

Sighing, he took a deep breath and eyed the chocolate sitting on his lap. Each bar was different. There was dark chocolate, chocolate with sea salt, chocolate caramel, and chocolate with almonds. Dark chocolate had always been Gloria's favorite so he decided to eat that in honor of her. Picking up the dark chocolate bar, he placed the other three on the coffee table. Heather could select one of the other three when she arrived home tonight.

Feeling a combination of sadness that his wife couldn't join him in this treat and joy in knowing that their life had been special, he opened the bar. The smell of chocolate filled his nostrils and he eagerly took a big bite. Jake was right, it was soft and beginning to melt. He made a mental note to place the other three in the refrigerator when he finished his bar.

He relaxed and leaned against the back cushions,

relishing his treat. He didn't indulge in sweet treats very often, preferring the salty variety, popcorn being his favorite. Today was an exception.

Jerry was half-way through the bar when he frowned and looked down to study it. Rubbing his stomach, he belched, throwing up a little in his mouth. He swallowed then slowly set the candy bar on the arm of the sofa. He blinked a couple of times and shook his head, trying to dispel the fuzziness. Standing was out of the question, he was too dizzy. He searched the room trying to find his cell phone. He tried lifting his arms but they weren't following his commands. Instead, he inched them up to feel his pants pockets in case his phone was there. No luck.

Having been a Weehawkin cop for thirty years, and knowing his body, it didn't take him long to realize that he had been drugged, probably from the chocolate since that was the only thing he had eaten since breakfast. He reached for the pad and pen that were on the coffee table but the motion carried him forward and he crumpled to the carpet, hitting his head on the coffee table. Lying on his side, such as he was, it vaguely registered that the fingernails on his left hand were turning blue. Groaning, he vomited then closed his eyes.

You were right about the phone, son was Jerry's last thought before he lost consciousness.

CHAPTER SEVEN

Penthouse Suite
Thursday, January 6, 5:08 p.m.

MALI AND JAKE walked into their room after spending the afternoon jet skiing all over the bay.

"We have to do that somewhere on the east coast this summer. That was awesome and Heather would love it," exclaimed Mali as she set her bag down on a chair.

"I still can't believe that was your first time. You handled it like a pro. I especially liked it when you turned too sharply and flew off. I didn't see your face but I can imagine how you looked." Jake threw back his head and laughed.

Mali smacked him on his arm. "Oh you. I only made that mistake once. The rest of the time, I stayed right with you."

Jake nodded. "You did indeed. You can jet ski in New York Harbor, by the way."

"New York Harbor? Really?" When he nodded, she added, "That would be incredible to jet ski close to the Statue of Liberty. Can you do that?"

Jake picked her up and swung her around. "Your wish is my command, wife. We will make it happen." He let her slide down his body and kissed her soundly.

"Hmmmm...I like, husband of mine. Do that again."

"Happy to oblige." He kissed her again and was backing her up to the couch when the hotel phone rang.

When Mali moved to end the kiss, Jake shook his head, still kissing her.

"Don't answer that."

She ended the kiss. "It could be about our flight home tomorrow. I called the front desk when you were in the restroom before we left to inquire about a car."

Jake sighed and stepped out of her way. By that time, the phone had stopped ringing. Mali giggled and shook her head when she saw the hopeful look in Jake's eye. She walked to the kitchen, picked up the hotel phone sitting on the counter, and dialed zero for the front desk.

"Hola. How can I help you?" asked the attendant.

"Hi. This is Mali Black. Someone just called for us."

There was a pause and Mali heard some shuffling of papers.

"Oh yes, Señora Black. We've been trying to reach you for some time now. A man by the name of Paul Santini said he's been trying to reach Señor Black on his cell phone but no one answers. He says it's extremely important."

Mali's eyes shot to Jake who narrowed his eyes and cocked his head to the side. "We've been out all afternoon. We'll call Mr. Santini right now. Thank you." She hung up the phone.

As soon as he heard Paul's name, Jake had rushed to the bedroom.

Mali ran to the room.

"There are several messages from Paul. I'm calling him right now." He didn't look up when he spoke but she could hear the alarm in his voice.

"Paul, it's Jake." As he listened to Paul, he sank to the bed. Mali rushed over and sat next to him, one hand on his leg and the other rubbing his back.

Jake's voice was thick with emotion. "We'll be on the next flight out. Where is Heather?" Jake nodded. "Good. Thank you, Paul, for everything. I'll text you with our flight information and will confirm our approximate arrival time at the hospital." He paused. "Thanks. I'll call them as soon as I get it."

He hung up the phone. His tears tore at her heart. She pulled him close, tearing up herself. He squeezed her tight then pulled back.

"Dad's in the hospital." He swiped at his tears, grimacing. "Paul went over there to pick up the stuff for their fishing trip and found him unconscious on the floor in the living room. It looked like he had eaten some chocolate then had thrown up. Paul thought it might be an allergic reaction to the chocolate. He called 911 right away."

As he was talking, Mali had walked over to the nightstand on her side of the bed to pick up her cell.

"Dad's not allergic to chocolate." He looked at Mali, concern etched on his face. "They're not telling him much since he's not family. He's texting me the hospital number."

"And Heather?"

"She was at a friend's house for a play date and will spend the night there. Ah, Paul's text just came in."

"Call the hospital while I phone my father. We need a jet, fast, and he can make it happen."

With grateful eyes, Jake stood and stepped onto the patio to make his call.

Mali dialed her father's number.

"Hello Jasmine. I didn't expect to hear from you this week," he chuckled.

"Father, Jerry was found unconscious in the house and was taken to a hospital. We need to leave for New Jersey as soon as possible and we need to get there fast."

All business, Charles responded. "Let me make a few calls. I'll arrange for a jet to be waiting at the Cabo airport and for a car to pick you up at the hotel to take you there. I'll call back in fifteen minutes." He hung up without waiting for a reply.

Jake strode back into the bedroom as Mali was pulling out the suitcases. She paused when she saw the look on his face.

"He overdosed."

"What?"

"They don't know what drug it is at this point, but it's potent. They're trying to keep his organs from shutting down. Oh, God, he's on a ventilator and it doesn't look good." He dropped his phone on the bed as Mali flew into his arms. He held onto her as if his life depended on it while she repeated words of comfort.

She finally pulled away to update him and to give him something to do.

"Father is calling back in a few minutes. He's arranging for a car to pick us up and take us to the airport where a jet will be waiting." He stared at her without moving. "Jake, we need to pack right now." He blinked a few times then nodded and moved to the closet.

They packed efficiently and quickly. Jake was zipping up the first suitcase when Mali's phone rang.

"Jasmine, a car will be there in ten minutes. A jet is flying down from San Diego and should be there in an hour."

"Thank you, Father. You're on speaker with us."

"Hello Jacob. I'm sorry to hear about Jerry. How is Heather?"

"Heather had evidently gone to a friend's house for a play date after school and wasn't home. Dad's other friend, George, waited at our house for their return. He made arrangements for Heather to stay at her friend's house until we get home and can pick her up."

"What more can we do?"

"You're already doing so much for us, sir. I—"

Mali interrupted him. "Actually, would it be possible for you and Mother to come to New Jersey? We're not sure how long we'll be at the hospital, and having you there would be a big help."

"We'll head there first thing in the morning. Call if you run into any problems and also when you get to the hospital."

"Thank you, Father."

"Your Mother is texting the information you'll need at the airport. Safe travels back. We're praying for Jerry."

When the call ended, Mali used the hotel phone on the nightstand to inform them that they were checking out a day early. A porter was sent up to collect their bags and it wasn't long before they were in the car speeding toward the airport.

An hour and a half later, they were in the air.

* * *

Hoboken University Medical Center
ICU
Friday, January 7, 3:20 a.m.

Jake and Mali hurried into the hospital, meeting Paul and George at the entrance as they had previously arranged. After hugging both, Paul led them to the ICU.

Paul and George could best be described as crotchety. They were always together, more often than not with Jerry in tow, and they bickered like an old married couple. Both were single and short, slightly stooped, standing no higher than Jake's chest. Paul sported a bushy gray beard that matched the curly mop on his head and he was constantly swiping hair from his eyes. George, on the other hand, was bald by choice. When he discovered that he was losing his hair at the age of thirty-two, he decided to be done with it and shaved it all off. The three friends, who had known each other since childhood, had a shaving party at the time, and celebrated each swipe of the razor with a shot of tequila.

They still laughed about it today, especially if George let too much time pass between shavings.

"Thanks for staying at the hospital," began Jake.

"He'd do the same for us," uttered George. "We've been praying all night."

Jake smiled his thanks.

As they approached the ICU, Jake excused himself to ask for a doctor and update while Mali, Paul, and George stepped into the deserted waiting room. They had just taken a seat when Jake walked in to join them.

"The nurse said dad was hanging on. She's going to have the on-call doctor come by soon." He paused. "Tell me what happened."

Paul responded. "I left a message for Jerry that I was going to stop by to pick up the food he bought for our fishing trip tomorrow. It's Friday now, right?" He peeked at his watch and nodded once. "It was about six o'clock, I guess. We were supposed to have a beer and a chat before Heather returned home." He sniffed. "I enjoy seeing Heather, she's such a light in all our lives." Jake squeezed Paul's shoulder.

Turning his head to look at Mali, he added, "Jerry told me last night…well, it was Wednesday night. He told me that Heather was spending the next day, that would be yesterday, Thursday, with her friend after school and wouldn't be home until after dinner." He sighed. "Anyway, when I got to the house and knocked, there was no answer. The door was unlocked so I opened it and went inside. Jerry was in the living room, lying on the floor. Chocolate bars were sitting on the coffee table and one was partially eaten on the arm of the sofa. I went over to him. He was unconscious. I put my ear to his chest and felt him breathing but he didn't look good and I couldn't wake him up." He stopped and used his handkerchief to wipe his eyes. "I called 911 then George." He sniffed again.

George picked up where Paul ended. "I got there as fast as I could but I was in the garden when Paul called. It took me a few minutes to go inside to get my keys and wallet. By the time I arrived, they were putting Jerry in the ambulance. Paul told me to stay at the house until Heather arrived home then he went with Jerry in the ambulance. I went inside. I didn't touch nothing." He glanced at Jake. "I figured with your line of work, it was probably best that I left things alone."

Jake nodded. "I appreciate that, George."

"Jerry had built a fire, it was cold today, so I tamped it down and secured it then sat in a chair by the window. When a car pulled up, I stepped outside and stopped everyone from going in until I could speak with the woman who brought Heather home. A Janny Colton, I think she said?"

"Janine Colton, yes. Her daughter, Becca, and Heather are the best of friends."

"Ah, she told the girls to wait in the car for a few minutes while she spoke with me. I explained what happened and she offered to keep Heather until you came home. The girls are about the same size. Ms. Colton said Heather could wear some of Becca's clothes. She told me to tell you that she's praying for Jerry and will be vague with Heather about why she's spending the night at their house. She said to call when you want her to bring Heather home."

"Thanks, George, I appreciate that. And thank you, Paul, for getting an ambulance to the house as fast as you did."

Paul's body was shaking as he tried to hold back the tears. "I should have gone there earlier. Maybe I could have helped more."

Mali left the chair she was sitting in and walked over to Paul, sitting down on the couch between George and him. She took his wrinkled, arthritic hand in hers. "Paul, don't do that to yourself. We don't know what happened, and to think you could have prevented it is flawed thinking and will only make you feel worse. You could be lying in this hospital alongside Jerry had you arrived earlier. We just don't have all the facts yet. You did everything you could and we are grateful."

Paul patted her hand.

"Mali's right, Paul. I—"

At that moment, a young male doctor strode into the room. He was wearing blue scrubs with a white lab coat over it and a stethoscope around his neck.

"Jacob Black?" When Jake turned to him, he said, "I'm Dr. Arun Ramisted. I've been with your father since his arrival. Let's have a seat." He motioned to three empty chairs.

Mali took the seat next to Jake. The doctor sat across from them.

"This is my wife, Mali."

The doctor acknowledged Mali before turning his eyes back to Jake. "Your father overdosed on fentanyl."

"What?" Both Jake and Mali responded. Paul gasped and George looked confused but didn't say anything.

"We pumped his stomach which only contained chocolate. We believe whatever chocolate he ate was laced with the drug."

Jake leaned back in the chair. "My God."

"Fentanyl is incredibly potent, more so than heroin. Two milligrams, roughly four grains of salt, can kill an adult. He obviously didn't ingest that amount or he wouldn't be with us right now."

Jake swallowed. "Did pumping his stomach remove all of the drug?"

"No. Normal protocol for an opioid overdose is naloxone. We administered one dose, pumped his stomach, then administered a second dose. While we didn't know the specific drug at the time of his arrival, we were able to quickly determine that it was an overdose."

"Did the naloxone work? Is my dad going to be all right?"

The doctor looked straight in to Jake's eyes. "Mr. Black, unfortunately, too much time has passed between the time your father ingested the fentanyl and when we administered the naloxone. His organs were already beginning to shut down when he arrived. We have been working to reverse that, to no avail thus far."

Jake reached for Mali's hand, enveloping it in his and squeezing tight.

"He is on a ventilator to help him breathe and we

continue to monitor him. I'm sorry to say that his chance of survival is very low."

Jake swallowed and looked down at their connected hands. "Can we see him?"

"Of course. I'll take you and your wife to his room. Before we go, I need to tell you that I am required by law to notify the authorities when there are drug overdoses, and the circumstances surrounding them. I know your father was a police officer in Weehawken and I thank him for his service. Out of respect for him, I have waited for your arrival before contacting them. They will go to your home to conduct an investigation. In addition, given that fentanyl is such a dangerous drug that can even be absorbed through the skin, the local fire department will be dispatched to sanitize the house. Someone needs to be there to let them in and I can't stress how important it is not to touch anything."

Mali's eyes darted to Paul and George then back at the doctor. "His friend, Paul," she pointed to him, "found Jerry and went over to him to check his pulse and to help. And George was in the house later tamping down the fire, although he didn't touch any of the chocolate or anything else. I would feel more comfortable if both could be examined."

The doctor eyed the two men and nodded. "Of course. Given how they look and the fact that they feel all right..." Both men nodded. "I doubt they are in danger. But it's always good to ensure there are no minute traces in their systems. I'll send a nurse to collect them. Let me take you to your father now."

Jake and Mali followed the doctor to the intensive care unit. Given the nature of his overdose, he was in a room by himself. Out of an abundance of caution, Jake and Mali dressed in sterile blue surgical gowns with gloves and they wore a mask covering their nose and mouth with a plastic face shield over it. Dr. Ramisted added the face mask and shield for himself then slid gloves on before pushing the door open to step inside.

Mali paused just inside the door, letting Jake walk to the bed ahead of her. She covered her mouth with her hand, tears leaking from her eyes.

Numerous monitors surrounded the head of the single hospital bed. An IV was in Jerry's left arm, attached to two bags of fluids that were hanging on a stand. A tube had been inserted down his throat, secured to his mouth with tape. The rhythmic whoosh-pause of the ventilator echoed in the room, the sound of the beeping monitors a mere whisper.

He looked frail and small.

Jake picked up Jerry's hand as he gazed at him, swallowing numerous times. "Surely there's something more you can do for him, doctor," he said thickly.

The doctor put down the chart he had picked up to study. He shook his head. "I wish there was, Mr. Black. The rest is up to your father and to God. I'm sorry." He walked over to Jake. "I'll be in the hospital all morning if you need anything."

Jake nodded without looking up. "Thank you."

Mali set her purse down on the single chair and joined Jake at Jerry's bedside. She placed her left hand on Jake's back and gazed down at her father-in-law. Jake told his father how much he loved him and how much he appreciated everything he did for the two of them. He spoke of Heather's love for her Papa, reminiscing about their life together. Mali quietly listened, occasionally rubbing Jake's back, smiling at some of the stories he told.

At ten minutes to four, Jerry Black died, Jake and Mali by his side.

CHAPTER EIGHT

MALI UNLOCKED THE door to Jake's– to *their* house. She was numb, only returning home at his request even though she wanted to stay with him at the hospital.

"I need you to go to the house, take pictures, and gather whatever information you can before the police arrive," he had told her. "Once they begin their investigation, we won't have access to anything, at least for the foreseeable future." He kissed her and pulled her into his arms, whispering, "I want you here too, but I need you there more right now." He pulled back to look down into her eyes. "I need to find out what the hell is going on and who did this to dad. I don't trust anyone but you to look at the details."

She brushed the hair from his forehead and placed her hand on his cheek. The pain in his eyes was almost more than she could bear. "All right."

"Be careful, don't touch anything with your bare hands." He kissed her nose. "I love you."

"I love you, too."

Mali set her purse on the table by the front door and turned to the living room. Standing at the entrance, she took a deep breath as she looked around. The tears had dried but she was still in a fog as she tried to focus. Giving herself a mental shake, she walked upstairs to the master bedroom and continued on to the bathroom. Pulling a hand towel off the rack, she opened cabinet doors and drawers, and finally found what she was looking for. Grabbing two plastic gloves, she turned and walked back downstairs, pulling the gloves on as she did so.

She picked up her phone and snapped a few pictures of the living room from the entrance. She edged closer to the sofa and coffee table where the chocolate bars were, taking pictures from various angles. The box was sitting next to the bars. She snapped pictures of the chocolate bars then picked up the box with the thumb and forefinger of her left hand. The box had no return address but it did have a few stickers on it. She captured photos of all sides then set the box back down. She continued taking photos of anything she believed was relevant. Pausing, she looked down at the chocolate and nodded once, making a decision. Turning around, she walked into the kitchen and to a drawer next to the pantry. Opening it, she found a gallon ziplock bag then returned to the living room. She picked up the untouched chocolate bar that was on top of the stack and put it into the bag, then peeled off the glove that had picked it up, placing it in the bag inside out. She was just turning toward her purse when the doorbell rang. Startled, she rushed to her purse and placed the bag inside, then removed the other glove from her hand and shoved it into her pocket as she walked to the front door.

"Good morning, ma'am," said an older officer. "I'm Officer Jenkins and this is Detective Harrison." He pointed to a much younger man standing next to him. Both showed their credentials to Mali. She glanced past them to the black sedan beyond then shifted her attention back to them. "I worked with Jerry the last two years he was on the force. I'm very sorry for your loss."

"Thank you. The doctor at the hospital said you'd be coming here to investigate."

"Yes ma'am. We'd like to come inside."

"Of course." Mali stepped aside and allowed them entry.

"Has anything been touched?"

Mali shook her head. "Not to my knowledge."

"Good. It's cold outside so I won't ask you to leave. But I need you to remain by the front door. Forensics will be here momentarily as well as the fire department. They will remove all traces of drugs and sanitize the place."

Mali remained by the door as they worked, opening the door for forensics when they arrived.

Shortly after seven, Mali's phone rang.

"Jasmine, it's your father. We're here, they won't let us near the house."

"I'll be right out." She had contacted them with the news about Jerry earlier as she left the hospital.

Mali excused herself and walked outside, down the path to the wrought iron gate. She looked to her left and right. When she spotted her parents, who were both standing outside the car, she opened the gate and ran to them. Her mother embraced her and told her how sorry she was to hear of Jerry's passing.

"Jacob is still at the hospital?" her father asked.

Mali nodded. "There's paperwork and stuff he has to take care of. I don't expect him back for a while. Jerry's friends, Paul and George, are still there as well."

"When was the last time you ate?"

"I'm not sure, Mother, on the jet that brought us here I guess, although I wasn't hungry."

"You need to eat." Mali began to object but Willow cut her off. "Jasmine, you will need your strength to deal with the next few days and to help Jake with Heather."

"Oh God, Heather will be crushed."

"Let us take you to breakfast and perhaps they'll be done here by the time we return."

Mali rubbed her face. "All right. Let me tell the detectives that I'll be back in an hour." She went back to the house, disappearing inside for a few minutes before returning to her parent's car.

By the time they drove back to the house, Mali noticed a black sedan with the letters DEA on the side. Jake was home and was talking with the detectives and fire department as well as a DEA agent. He was in full FBI-mode. After speaking with Jake, the detectives, forensics, and fire department finished their work and left shortly after eleven in the morning, all traces of chocolate and any potential dangers removed from the house. The DEA agent followed the others shortly after.

Willow and Charles were sitting at the dining table

with Mali and Jake, all drinking coffee, when Heather ran inside. Jake stood as soon as he heard her enter.

"You're home!" Laughing, she threw herself into Jake's arms. "I've missed you so much. I can't wait to tell you all about my week." She looked over her dad's shoulder and saw Mali as well as Willow and Charles. She gasped in delight. "Mommy! And Papa two and Grammy are also here!" She jumped down from her dad's arms and ran to give Mali a hug and kiss then raced around the table to hug Willow and Charles. Turning her head left then right, she asked, "Where's Papa?"

Jake and Mali looked at each other then at Heather. Mali's hands, which were resting on her lap, closed into fists. Willow and Charles excused themselves and walked into the kitchen as Jake picked up Heather and sat down with her on his lap.

8:30 p.m.

Jake walked into the kitchen where Mali was wiping the counters. Willow and Charles were sitting on stools at the counter sipping red wine.

"She's finally asleep." Jake rubbed his eyes then accepted a glass of wine from Mali before moving to the counter.

Mali poured herself a glass then joined the other three. "Before leaving this afternoon, Father Jameson said we should stop by the church tomorrow morning at nine to finalize details."

"I'm glad he can accommodate our request for the viewing tomorrow evening and the funeral on Sunday afternoon."

Mali squeezed his shoulder as she sat down next to him. "I'm not surprised considering how long they knew each other."

He sighed. "Lord, I'm tired."

Willow said, "Jake, Charles and I have been talking. We want to take Heather home with us after the funeral and have her stay with us for a few days."

Jake frowned. "She needs me, especially now. This is going to remind her of when her mother died. She needs Mali too."

"We understand that, and we recognize that you're both torn between finding out who did this and helping Heather."

Charles spoke up. "Jake, we would enjoy having her with us, you won't have to worry about her. Besides, you know you want to focus on catching whoever did this. Both of you will be consumed with it."

While listening to the exchange, Mali noticed the flashing light on the phone's answering machine. She walked over to the machine and pressed play. There were two new messages, one from Paul and the second from another friend of Jerry's. Mali was about to stop the machine when an old message played.

"Hi Dad. Just wanted to let you know that we sent you a little something from Cabo. It may melt so open it right away. We hope you and Heather enjoy it. See you tomorrow. Love you Dad."

"What the ?" The stool Jake was sitting on slammed to the floor as he shot up. He was at the machine in an instant. He played the message again, while looking at Mali. "This isn't me."

She was staring at him with concern. "I know."

Willow frowned and looked from one to the other. "I don't understand. It sounds like you."

"It's not me." He looked down at the counter briefly before lifting his head to stare at Mali.

"I still don't understand. What does this mean?" asked Willow, looking from one to the other.

Jake didn't answer Willow directly. "It's not safe here. We'll check into a hotel first thing in the morning before we meet with Father Jameson."

Mali nodded.

"And I want the team updated and in the office by six Monday morning."

"I'll contact Kirsten and Joe. I need to talk to them anyway, Sara too." Mali picked up her cell and walked into the living room.

Jake looked over at Charles. "I think it's a very good idea for Heather to go with you."

Charles nodded. "We'll arrange for extra security at the house as well."

"I appreciate that."

* * *

St. Lawrence Roman Catholic Church
Weehawken, NJ
Sunday, January 9, 2:30 p.m.

Heather tugged on Mali's hand. When Mali knelt down so she was eye level with her, Heather whispered, "I'm scared to see him."

"Oh honey." Mali picked Heather up, stood, and walked down the middle aisle toward the altar. Heather buried her face in Mali's neck, crying with the occasional hiccup, her arms squeezing Mali's neck. When she reached the front pew on the left side of the aisle, Mali sat down with Heather in her lap, rocking her from side to side. "Let's just sit for a while." Charles and Willow sat to Mali's left. Her concerned eyes met Jake's as he was speaking with Father Jameson.

They had arrived at the church early because Jake wanted to speak with the priest and spend a few minutes alone with his dad, who was lying in rest before the altar in an open casket.

The Rosary was held in a smaller room the night before and this was Mali's first time inside the main room of the church. Despite the circumstances, she admired what she saw. The church was small and quaint with two sets of pews that faced a simple altar. On the wall behind the altar, a life-size painting of Christ, standing with his arms spread wide in welcome, was in the center on a white background. The remainder of the wall, on both sides of the white background, was made of the same soft brown-colored brick that was outside. Wood beams crisscrossed on the ceiling above, all leading to the spired top in the center of the building.

After a few minutes, Mali kissed the top of Heather's head. "I'm going to go pay my respects to Papa. Do you want to come with me?"

Heather shook her head without looking up. "Can you go then come back and tell me how he looks?" Her voice cracked and was raspy from crying.

"Of course."

"Come to Grammy, Heather." Willow reached for Heather and gathered her in her arms.

Mali walked over to the casket where Jake now stood, head bent, his hand inside the open casket on his father's shoulder. She placed her hand on Jake's shoulder as she stepped beside him. Sliding her hand down Jake's arm, she grasped his hand. He gripped it tightly and pulled her closer to his side, still looking at his dad.

"Ever since I was a small kid, I remember Dad saying 'Jacob, there's a feeling of God in this church.' He later told me that's the reason why he came week in and week out. He wanted to feel the hand of God."

Mali sniffed and cleared her throat. "It gives me great comfort knowing he's with God now, watching over all of us."

They stood there in silence for a few more minutes, then Mali returned to the pew.

As she sat down, Heather looked up from Willow's neck, her tear-streaked face breaking Mali's heart. "How did Papa look?"

Mali wiped a tear from Heather's cheek before

cupping her chin with her hand. "He looked like he was sleeping peacefully."

Heather pressed her lips together, shifting her eyes to stare at the casket and her father standing before it. "Daddy is so sad."

"Yes, he is."

"Maybe I'll go make sure he's okay."

"Do you want me to go with you?"

When Heather nodded, Mali stood and held out her hand. As they reached Jake's side, he looked down at Heather and held his arms open wide.

"Daddy."

He picked her up and held her close as the three said their goodbyes.

As with the Rosary, the funeral service went by in a blur for Mali. All of their friends, as well as many police officers with whom Jerry worked plus their entire FBI team, had piled inside for the service. There were many tears, some laughter as stories about Jerry were shared, and more offers of condolence than Mali could count. By the time they left for the cemetery, Mali was exhausted. She noticed that Heather and Jake were as well, and figured life would be that way for a while.

Mali was moved to tears when, as they drove the three miles to the cemetery, they observed both sides of the street lined with officers. Jerry was a fixture in the Weehawken community and it was never more apparent than this day.

Later that night in the hotel, Mali and Jake sat down to discuss plans with Charles and Willow.

"We're leaving early tomorrow morning to go to the office, probably before you're awake and definitely before Heather wakes up."

Charles and Willow nodded. "We figured you'd be out of here early."

"Thanks again for taking Heather with you. A change of scenery will be good for her right now. She told me tonight that she was looking forward to sleeping in her Mommy's room."

"I'll be sure to put some of Jasmine's things in there. I still have the comforter that you loved." Willow smiled.

Mali eyes popped open wide. She had no idea her mother kept anything sentimental. Without commenting on that, she said, "We're going to stay at the apartment in town for the foreseeable future. Don't tell anyone where we are–"

"And don't tell anyone that Heather is with you," interrupted Jake.

"I've already lined up additional security for the grounds and inside the house."

"Thank you, Charles. Until we figure out who did this to dad, we have to assume that everyone in the family is at risk. Please be careful."

CHAPTER NINE

Special Unit Warehouse
Undisclosed Location, New York
Monday, January 10, 6:10 a.m.

"GOOD MORNING, EVERYONE," said Jake, looking from one team member to another. They were all standing at the control center, their technical hub and informal meeting locale. "First of all, thank you for going to dad's funeral yesterday. I…*we*," Jake looked at Mali before continuing, "appreciated that more than you know." He took a deep breath. "Now, down to business." He turned to Joe, handing him the recording from the answering machine. "Download this recording."

"Sure thing." Joe worked his magic, signaling to Jake when he was ready. At Jake's nod, he pressed a button to play the recording. Everyone listened to it then looked to Jake for an explanation.

"Dad received this message the same morning that the chocolate laced with fentanyl arrived." He paused, taking a sip of coffee. "I didn't call dad. The voice is not mine."

"What?" Kirsten's eyebrows shot up as she leaned forward.

Felix's eyes opened wide. "No kidding!"

"Sure sounds like you," exclaimed Joe.

Jeff scratched his beard with his hand. "Shit!"

"Is there any way we can break the voice down to get to the real voice?" asked Mali.

Felix became animated. "There are a variety of voice-altering software, one in particular that I'm thinking of, that—"

"This isn't a digital representation of a voice," interrupted Jeff, shrugging when Felix glared at him. "That kind of software won't help."

"Not directly, but we may be able to reverse engineer it, fool it into thinking that it's not a real voice. It's worth a try."

Jake held his hand up. "Before we start trying to solve anything, I want to identify what it is that we need to solve. There's much more involved than the voice recording."

Everyone nodded as Mali walked over to the conference table area to grab a white board and roll it over to the group. After positioning it for everyone to see, she pulled the cap off the black pen and started to make a list. "Is there a way to break down the voice recording to the true voice? Who made the call? Where did the call come from? How does this tie to Jake?"

"Hoop, give Joe the pictures you took of the box and everything," said Jake.

She reached into her pocket and pulled out a flash drive, handing it to Joe.

Joe placed one picture on each of the nine large screens on the back wall. "There are more pictures. These are the first nine."

"Good," said Jake as everyone studied the screens.

"Starting with the top three pictures of the living room," began Mali, "note that everything is untouched. The only new element added to the room is the box that the candy arrived in and the candy bars, all sitting on the coffee table with the exception of a partially eaten chocolate bar on the arm of the sofa. The doctor confirmed that the fentanyl he ingested was in the chocolate he ate, not in something else that was in the house. Moving on, the middle three pictures show a closer look of the candy and box sitting on the table from various angles."

"Is the chocolate from Mexico?" asked Susan. Susan Walker, the last member of the team, was a security specialist who joined the team a few months prior when they were pursuing Janet Simpson.

"Good question. You can see from the bottom three pictures and the next three..." Mali paused to tell Joe, "Move to the next nine pictures."

The screens flashed then changed to nine new pictures.

"At the top of the screen, the front and back of the wrapping paper of the three bars on the coffee table look like they're from Mexico but there's no way to determine if the chocolate actually came from Mexico or from somewhere else."

Jake added, "Hoop was careful to replace everything she picked up exactly where she found it knowing the police and DEA would show up shortly after her arrival at the house. Everything was taken by the DEA as evidence, well, almost everything. We'll try to get answers to some of our questions but it may not be timely, if they even decide to cooperate with us."

"Almost everything?" asked Joe.

Mali picked up her purse, that was hanging on the chair closest to her, and held up a baggie with the chocolate bar inside.

Kirsten gasped.

"You took it?" asked Jeff.

"Darn right I did." Mali set the baggie on the corner of the control center. "We can have this chocolate tested and perhaps get at least one answer without needing the DEA." She turned and wrote the additional question about the origin of the chocolate on the white board.

"Awesome!" exclaimed Kirsten. She continued to stare at the pictures. "There's no address on the box other than Jerry's name and address. Where did the box come from?"

"One of the questions that we need to answer," replied Jake and Mali wrote it down.

"Let's take a closer look at the box," said Mali. "Joe, zoom in on the first picture, please, and then we'll do the same for each of the six pictures."

Susan frowned as she observed the top of the box where Jerry's name and address were located. "In addition to no return address, there's no postage. Who delivered it? UPS? FedEx?"

"Unknown at this point," answered Jake.

They continued going through the pictures, with Mali writing each question down.

"What are those small stickers?" asked Joe as he zoomed in on three located on one side in the bottom left corner. Mali had taken a picture of the side of the box with the three stickers in a row, her pinky finger next to it, so they'd have a general idea of the size of each. Two were the same size, the first one was larger.

Felix, who had been silent since they began studying the pictures, jumped into the conversation. "That first sticker on the far left with the three lollipops looks familiar to me. I've seen it somewhere."

Jake nodded. "Good. We'll assign duties once we finish going through the pictures and have a more complete list of questions."

The team spent the next hour going through all pictures. Finally, Jake signaled a break. "Let's take twenty to refresh our coffees and take care of other business. We'll return with fresh eyes to make sure we haven't missed anything. We'll assign tasks just before we break for lunch."

"Things are going well," stated Mali. "This is a good list of questions." They were both facing the white board and studying the questions.

Jake rubbed his neck and shook his head. "Too many, and we're flying blind since we're not running the investigation. Speaking of..." He stood straighter and reached for his phone. "I need to call Special Agent Hernandez."

Special Agent-in-Charge Rose Hernandez was a

hard core, by-the-book agent who had stepped in as the agent-in-charge when their previous boss, Frank Grant, was killed by Janet Simpson's assassin a few months ago. She ran things differently than Frank and they were still getting used to her way of doing things. The team did not have as much autonomy as they did when Frank was alive, a source of frustration for them.

Jake squeezed her hand then walked to the conference table and sat down to make his call.

Mali walked to her computer station and logged in to her account then began going through her numerous emails that she had not seen since before the wedding.

"How are you two holding up?" asked Kirsten, ten minutes later. She handed Mali a diet coke, sipping one herself.

"Thanks for this," Mali said, as she took a sip. "I needed the cold caffeine." She took another long sip. "To answer your question, we're doing all right. It all still feels surreal until we go to say something to Jerry and realize he's not there. Jake is handling things, he's very stoic. Solving his dad's murder will help with closure. I hope we can solve it quickly."

* * *

The team had just gathered together when Special Agent Hernandez strode into the room. "A word, Agent Black?" Without waiting for him to follow, she turned and walked back to the elevator.

"Excuse me." Jake followed Agent Hernandez to the elevator where the two spoke quietly.

Mali was standing next to the white board that listed the questions. She held an iPad in her hand. "Joe, could you display this information for me?" She swiped up on her iPad and moments later the top middle screen flashed and an image displayed. "Display it on all nine screens for the largest possible image."

Joe nodded and all screens blinked before displaying the image on all nine as one big picture.

"I did some basic research on fentanyl while sitting in the hospital. I'm sure everyone has heard about the exponentially increased use of fentanyl and corresponding opioid overdoses and deaths in this country."

Everyone nodded.

"It's horrible," uttered Susan, biting her lip.

"Fentanyl is especially lethal. It's a synthetic drug, manmade in laboratories, typically used to manage pain after certain surgeries and with some cancers. It has made its way to the illicit drug market because it's easy and cheap to produce, and is extremely potent. Street names include China Town, China White, Dance Fever, Goodfellas, and Great Bear. It's fifty to one hundred times more potent than heroin. You know those packets of salt you can get at fast food restaurants?" Everyone nodded. "If it was fentanyl, one packet would kill all of us plus a few more." Susan and Kirsten gasped. "It's also combined with drugs like heroin and cocaine. The drug dealer can make substantially more money by selling a product that's laced with fentanyl. Heavy users and recreational drug users become addicted to it or die from an overdose. And non-drug users who are taking pain meds after surgery could actually be taking fentanyl. In those cases, the user may never know that they're taking it but become addicted nonetheless."

"My God," stated Kirsten as she stared at the information.

"Given the flow of drugs coming in from our southern border, we are seeing a nationwide spike in fentanyl-related overdoses and deaths. It gets worse."

"How can it get worse?" asked Felix.

"Fentanyl can be added to virtually anything." Swiping her iPad, she asked Joe to display the new image.

The image was of chocolate, gummy bears, lollipops, and other miscellaneous candy. "As you know, Jerry ingested chocolate laced with fentanyl. Although most commonly produced in pill form to look like oxycodone and other prescription drugs or added to illicit drugs like heroin, candy is being laced with it. Teens and children are now in the cross-hairs of drug dealers."

"Horrible," said Jeff, shaking his head.

"What–" began Susan.

Jake's raised voice interrupted Susan and the team's focus shifted to Jake and Agent Hernandez. They were standing toe to toe, Agent Hernandez not backing down from Jake's rigid stance. Jaw clenched, his hands were fisted at his sides as he listened to whatever Agent Hernandez was saying to him. When she gestured to the group with her left arm, Jake turned his head and stared at Mali briefly before shaking his head as he returned his gaze back to her. Mali could tell by the rapid rise and fall of his chest that he was trying to control his anger.

Shifting her attention back to the team, Mali quietly said, "Let's all take a short break." Seeing the question in everyone's eyes, she just shrugged her shoulders.

"A break won't be necessary," said Agent Hernandez as she walked over to the group. "Gather your things and take the rest of the day off. Be back here tomorrow at o-seven-thirty." Confusion reigned but no one said a word as they turned to gather their things. "Agent Hooper, you will stay."

Frowning, Mali turned back to the control center.

Kirsten mouthed *call me* to Mali as she walked past her to the elevator, the others following quietly.

While Agent Hernandez watched everyone step inside the elevator, Mali pulled her flash drive from the control center, placing it in her pocket as she moved to shut everything down. She reached for the baggie with the chocolate bar.

Hearing her, Agent Hernandez shifted her eyes back to Mali. "Before you shut down the computer, send me a copy of those images then delete them." She looked down at Mali's hand. Eyes narrowing, she held out her hand. "I'll take that."

"What's going on, Agent Hernandez?" asked Mali, as she reluctantly handed the baggie to her. Jake had joined her, and she read the fury in his eyes when she glanced up at him.

"This is a DEA matter and I told Agent Black that the team will cease and desist all aspects of this case."

"What? Jake's father was killed by fentanyl!" Mali bristled. "We should be the ones handling this specific case. It'll get lost in the massive generic 'let's stop the drugs from coming into the country' angle that the DEA is pursuing. Have one of their agents assigned to our team to work with us."

Agent Hernandez was shaking her head before Mali even finished. "After Jake phoned me with his intentions, I called the DEA in DC to offer our assistance. They unequivocally said no, that they were in the middle of a critical element to their case regarding fentanyl-laced drugs, not the generic 'coming into the country' angle as you so eloquently put it, and they don't want anyone messing it up."

Mali gasped, outraged.

"Their words, not mine," she said, holding up her hand. She sighed, shaking her head. "I am not without compassion. I understand how important this is to you." She turned her stare to Jake. "Aside from the fact that the DEA said it's their case and does not want the FBI's assistance, you are too emotionally involved to handle this."

Jake's eyes squinted to narrow slits and his lips thinned again.

As he opened his mouth to say something, Mali interrupted. "The DEA may be pursuing fentanyl-laced drugs but it's in the pill form, which is more prevalent. I doubt they're pursuing the candy."

"And you know this, how?" Agent Hernandez crossed her arms. Mali pressed her lips together, not responding. "I thought so."

"This is an outrage and totally unacceptable! There is

no one better to handle this case, and get to the bottom of it, than Jake!" Glancing at him, she noticed a slight tilt up of the mouth before Agent Hernandez's words drew her attention.

"I thought you'd feel that way." She sighed as she looked from Jake to Mali. "Which is why, effective immediately, I'm placing you both on a two-week leave of absence."

Mali's mouth dropped open. "You're firing us?"

"I said leave of absence, Agent Hooper." Her words became hard as she lost her patience. "I suggest you take this time to grieve. Be with your daughter. Use the time wisely. Whatever you do, stay away from the office and this case. Let the DEA do their jobs. They'll find who-ever killed your father. Now, save the images then we'll all leave. I will write this off…" she held up the baggie "…as being overcome with grief."

"I have an empty flash drive at my cubicle."

Agent Hernandez nodded. "Everything else stays, including your laptop."

"Of course." Mali turned away, still fuming. With her back to Agent Hernandez, she winked at Jake as she passed him.

Jake distracted Agent Hernandez by asking about the rest of the team. Mali vaguely heard Agent Hernandez talk about a new case the team would start on tomor-row, but she was focused on her task. Leaning over, she quickly sent all related files that were on her laptop to her personal email before deleting them. She then closed all browser tabs and erased the browser history before shutting down her laptop. Opening the top drawer of her cubicle, she picked up an empty flash drive and held it up. "Here it is." She returned to the control center and saved the images to the drive, handing it to Agent Hernandez before deleting the images and shutting everything down.

All three walked to the elevator. While they waited for it, Agent Hernandez said, "I need both your credentials and ID passes to the building." She turned to Jake. "And I need your weapon."

CHAPTER TEN

Mali's apartment
5:45 p.m.

MALI AND JAKE walked into her apartment. By mutual consent, they had not spoken about what had occurred since leaving the warehouse, choosing instead to focus on matters like grocery shopping.

Mali's nose wrinkled. "It smells stale."

"Not surprising. It's been a couple of weeks since you were here." Jake closed the door and walked to the dining table, placing the supplies they purchased at Home Depot on it.

Mali walked into the kitchen and set the grocery bags she carried on the counter. As Jake left to grab their suitcases from the car, she unpacked the bags of food and put everything away. By the time he returned, she was pouring them each a glass of wine. Candles had been lit and their lavender scent was already filling the room.

She handed him a glass. "Let's leave the suitcases for later. I feel the need to sit on the balcony." She kissed Jake then walked through her bedroom to the sliding door, opened it, and stepped outside. She breathed deeply, admiring Jake when he joined her. He always looked like a panther to her, ready to strike. She clasped his hand in hers and they both sipped their wine, staring at the river.

Mali loved her apartment. It was on the ninth floor of the complex, right on the Hudson River. Modern rustic is how she liked to describe her place with its overstuffed sofa, oak furnishings, and earth tone rugs scattered across the hardwood floors. Warm landscape paintings complemented the feel. The kitchen was open to the living room with the focal point being the large picture windows overlooking the Hudson. Her bedroom was the only girly room in the apartment. Painted a pale rose, a white quilt with delicate tiny red roses embroidered along the hem covered the bed, and a small lamp on the nightstand gave a soft, muted glow to the room when it was on.

Her favorite spot, though, was the balcony. The sounds of the Hudson soothed her like no other place inside. Today was the exception. The sun bouncing off the water and the sound of the boats passing in the distance went unnoticed.

"I still can't believe what just happened." She leaned against the rail, twirling the wine glass in her hand and watching it swirl around. "I feel betrayed, somehow."

Jake had moved to the chair and was lounging in it with his legs stretched out in front of him. He rubbed his chin, his eyes following a speed boat as it passed. "Were you able to get all the information?"

She looked over her shoulder, grinning at him. "Is pigs ass pork?"

He barked out a laugh. Setting his glass on the table, he reached over and pulled Mali back until she sat on his lap. "Why Mrs. Black, where on earth did you hear that?"

"Kirsten has been known to say that on occasion." Mali giggled. "I don't know why that phrase popped into my mind."

Jake laughed again. "Thank you for defending me, by the way." He nuzzled the back of her neck. "We'll have to use the apartment as our base of operations."

Mali nodded as she tilted her head to the side for easier access. "Hmmmm." Breaking contact, she straightened and shifted to the side, studying Jake as she wagged her finger in front of him. She was all business now. "We won't get help from the team, officially, but Kirsten and the others will help in whatever way they can."

Jake sighed. "Okay." He sighed again then lifted her off his lap, before pushing out of the chair. "Let's eat and then set things up. I want to look at those pictures again."

After a quick dinner, they leaned two four-foot-by-three-foot white boards against the wall next to the television. Mali had written the questions the team had worked on earlier on one board, leaving the second one blank for the answers. Two other white boards, the same size, were set aside for later use. A large framed cork board was placed on the other side of the television with multiple tacks stuck into the upper right corner. Jake's laptop was sitting on the dining table next to Mali's printer and the other supplies they had purchased. Mali's laptop was on the coffee table and a long HDMI cord connected it to her television so they could view details on a larger screen.

Standing back, they assessed their set up.

"It's a good start." He paused, looking down at Mali. "If she finds out we're working the case on our own, we'll likely be fired, possibly worse."

Reaching her hand up to cup his cheek, she said, "Then we'd better work fast."

Jake smiled and lifted her hand from his cheek to kiss her palm. "Let's review the photos of the box again."

They both sat on the sofa and Mali plugged in the flash drive, bringing up the first photo. They studied it intently before moving on to the next one. No new questions came to mind until the photo of the bottom of the box displayed.

"No need to stop here, it's blank. Move on to the next."

Mali was about to click the mouse when a black smudge caught her eye. "What is that on the top right corner? A smudge of something?"

Jake squinted his eyes as Mali zoomed in. "I see it now. Good catch." He frowned. "I can't tell what it is. It could just be dirt."

The closer Mali zoomed in, the more blurred it became. "I don't think it's dirt. It could be a word or image but it's too grainy. Let me pull out a little, I might be able to sharpen it." She went into edit mode for the photo and made a few adjustments.

Jake walked to the television for a closer look. He nodded. "That's better. It's a word."

"Can you make out what is says? It looks like it starts with an R. There's an 'h' and an 'n'. Relaunch maybe? Rushing, like rushing the order?" She tried a few different possibilities then glanced at Jake when she realized he wasn't saying anything. Hands closed in fists, his body was coiled so tight, it looked like he would explode. "Jake?"

"Goddammit!" Without another word, Jake stormed through the bedroom and onto the balcony.

Stunned, Mali studied the box again before following Jake. He was sitting in a chair, elbows on his knees, lost in thought. She leaned against the sliding door.

"What does it say?"

Jake turned his head, his eyes cold. "*Revancha*. It means payback."

* * *

Mali remained silent as she walked over and sat down, waiting for Jake to continue.

He took a deep breath and let it out slowly. Grasping her left hand, he leaned toward her. "My last mission before leaving the Army a little over six years ago was in Mexico. Initially, I was tasked with locating and destroying the drug labs of the Los Rinches cartel. They had expanded their operations from the north central part of Mexico to include northeast Mexico, after taking over the Zetas cartel's territory when the leadership of that cartel were killed back in two thousand twelve. The move gave them control of the entire Texas border from El Paso to Brownsville, allowing the cartel to rapidly become one of the largest distributors of cocaine at the time, competing only with the Sinaloa Cartel that operates out of the northwest. The drug lord, Jose Armano, owned much of the police and the federales in the border cities and used a sophisticated system of transporting the drugs into our country. His network was immense. Their labs were spread throughout his territory but my focus was in the state of Chihuahua where the cartel began and where the largest labs were believed to be located. Armano's compound was located on the outskirts of the city of Madera, on the west side of the state. It would be an extra bonus to hit the labs closest to his compound, in his backyard as it were, and that was our goal. There were twelve men on my team, including myself, five Americans and seven indigenous soldiers familiar with the area."

"Was Jeff part of your team?"

"Spike? No. He was a part of the overall mission but was working in the Nuevo Leon state further west. Over the course of four weeks, my team successfully destroyed seven labs in and around Madera. A few smaller labs in Nuevo Leon were also destroyed. Between the two operations, we put a huge dent in Armano's bottom line. In retaliation, he attacked border agents working outside El Paso, brutally killing four men and hanging their bodies on trees across the Rio Grande from the U.S., to send a message. The message was received but the response was not what he expected. My team's mission changed. We were ordered to eliminate Armano. We organized and planned, watching the comings and goings of personnel, assessing the number of people within his compound, making sure we knew Armano's whereabouts within, that sort of thing. We breached it a week later in the early hours, taking out Armano and most of his soldiers. His wife and son escaped but, unfortunately, his two young daughters were killed. I was shot four times in the chest and abdomen, almost didn't make it."

"My God." She remembered the scars on his beautiful chest and teared up.

"It was during my recovery that we found out about my wife's cancer, at which point I resigned my commission and finished recuperating at home."

She cleared her throat. "I had no idea you were healing the same time you were taking care of Christa and Heather."

He brushed that aside, turning his head to ponder life as he focused on the water, as though seeking answers within its depths.

In the relative quiet, as she waited for Jake to continue, she tried to imagine what it must have been like for him. It was beyond her comprehension since she had not endured any hardships growing up.

Finally, tired of waiting of him to continue, she asked, "Do you think the cartel arranged to have your dad killed because of what happened six years ago? And, if so, why now and how did they find you?"

"I have no doubt that the message was for me." He paused. "We need to figure out what's going on, and quickly."

"Let's go to Agent Hernandez with this. Surely, it's grounds for us to be involved in the case."

"No." Jake shook his head. "She already believes I'm emotionally compromised." Mali's left eyebrow shot up. Jake exhaled through his nose, closing his eyes briefly before opening them. He shook his head. "Okay, I am. But I still believe we are in the best position to deal with this."

"All right. Let me see what I can find out about the cartel."

As they stood to return to the living room, Jake tugged on the hand he still held. When she looked at him, he added, "I don't want anyone to know about this, not even the team, at least until we have more information. You can tell them the basics of why we're on leave but that's it."

She nodded. "Kirsten asked me to call as she was leaving the office. I'll try to keep it generic." She squeezed his hand before releasing it. "We're going to get to the bottom of this, Jake." Her eyes turned cold. She waved her arm to emphasize what she was trying to say. "Then we'll find those responsible and take them out, or down, or, or whatever it is you say."

CHAPTER ELEVEN

JAKE STAYED IN the bedroom to make some calls while Mali stepped into the living room.

She dialed Kirsten's number, wanting to update her before beginning her research.

"It's about time you called," Kirsten said without preamble. "What the hell happened back there?"

"Agent Hernandez took the team off the case, made me erase all the photos and information we had collected. Then she sidelined Jake and I. We are officially on a two-week leave of absence."

Kirsten gasped. "That's bullshit!" Mali heard her tell Jen the news.

"I know. We're both furious. She thinks Jake is too emotionally compromised to do the job and the DEA doesn't want the FBI involved. She plans to put the team on a new case tomorrow."

"What are you going to do?"

Mali hesitated. Jake had just told her that he didn't want anyone to know what they were doing. "This is for your ears only, not even Jen, but we're going to continue working the case, quietly." She scrunched her nose, knowing Jake would not be pleased. But Kirsten was her best friend and would keep anything they discussed to herself, if asked.

"Hang on a sec." Mali heard her say something to Jen then the sound of the television faded away. A door squeaked then she heard the click of it closing. "Okay, I'm in the bedroom. Now, how can we help?"

"We were explicitly told to stay out of the DEA's way. We could get fired for what we're doing, and we don't want to put anyone on the team in a position where they could get fired too."

"Believe me, as soon as everyone hears what's going on, they'll be riled up and ready to help."

"We appreciate that, Kirsten, but we don't want anyone to lose their jobs over this. As it is, Jake won't be pleased that I'm giving you this much information. But, in all honesty, we need a little help to get the ball rolling." She paused, biting her lip as she considered whether or not to continue. "I need you to go into the office tomorrow at your usual early hour, snap a picture of the questions on the white board, and then erase them. Text me the image of the questions. I think I got them all when we set up here earlier, but I'm not one hundred percent sure. I erased all files on my laptop, per her orders, but I forgot to erase the board. Another thing, Felix said that he remembered seeing one of the stickers before. Can you call and ask him if he knows where he saw it? If not, maybe he can figure it out tonight before going into work tomorrow. Technically, the team doesn't know they're off the case yet."

"I'll call him as soon as we hang up. I'm going to call Joe as well. You might not want me to involve him, but he may be able to set up an algorithm to search for all of those stickers and send you a data dump before Hernandez arrives. As you said, technically we're not off the case yet. I'll make sure we act surprised when she tells us what's going on."

Mali chuckled. "Thanks. Gotta run."

"Take care, Mali. And be careful."

Mali sat down in front of her laptop to open the emails she sent from work that contained her initial research, and to organize her files. She could hear Jake speaking on the phone in the other room. The sound of his voice comforted her.

An hour later, Jake returned to the living room. "What have you found?"

"As you told me, Jose Armano's son, Carlos, escaped your raid on the compound with his mother. Despite being only sixteen at the time, he stepped into his father's role, changing the cartel since then into something more vicious and much more powerful from the looks of it. Here's an old picture I found of him." An image of a young man appeared on the television. He held a rifle in his arms and his feet were spread in a cocky stance, the cheeky grin on his face completing the look of confidence. He stood next to a tall woman with long black hair draped over her shoulder passing below her waist. Her hand was on the young man's shoulder and she was laughing at something. The picture was grainy making it difficult to see the details. "The woman is believed to be his mother. It's not the best picture. I'm hoping to find something better and more recent. Carlos has shifted the business from cocaine to fentanyl and is believed to be working with the Chinese to distribute it to the United States. That's all I have at this point."

"That's a good start but only creates more questions for us with no answers."

Mali walked over to the white boards that were set aside and picked one up, returning to the sofa. "I'm going to write all cartel-related questions on this board and we'll use the fourth for the answers."

Pulling the cap off the pen, she began writing as she voiced the questions out loud. "Did the cartel kill Jerry in retribution? If so, why now? How did they find Jake? Is the rest of the family a target? Where is Carlos Armano now? Is he working with the Chinese to distribute the fentanyl and how is it being distributed? How does Los Rinches work and where is their money?"

Looking at the questions, Jake said, "I called the former Army team I worked with six years ago. The only one I've kept in touch with off and on is Tim Jackson. He told me that both he and Ben Williams left the Army a year or two after me. They work for one of the government agencies on a contractual basis now. They don't have any information on the cartel but said that Carson Bole is still in the Army in Mexico and may have current intel. He told me that Eric Ingram, the fourth member, died in a car crash more than a year ago." He shook his head. "I wish I had known that."

To the list, Mali added, "Can Carson Bole provide us with current information on the cartel?"

"Tim and Ben are going to help. They're between jobs right now and will drive here as soon as they pick up some stuff."

Mali's eyebrows rose but she said nothing.

"It's getting late." Jake rubbed his eyes. "Let's call it a night and hit it tomorrow."

* * *

University of California group study room
Los Angeles
Tuesday, January 11, 1:30 a.m.

"Ugh, I'm exhausted." Cindy, a petite red-head with short cropped hair and deep blue Irish eyes, stretched her arms over her head, yawning. "This Pharmacology class is killing me. And our group is only dealing with the Alimentary tract and metabolism class of drugs. How are we going to learn all fourteen in one quarter?"

The team was sitting in a group study room within the graduate reading room of the Biomedical Library, the only area of the library that was open twenty-four hours every day for graduates to study.

"Quit grumbling," muttered Anna, Cindy's friend, equally petite but with a shaved head. She glanced at Cindy with tired brown eyes. "You were the one to convince me to become a nurse practitioner. I don't want to hear it."

Cindy threw her eraser at Anna, hitting her in the chest. Anna stuck her tongue out in return.

Pete, the leader of the group and the oldest at twenty-nine, was a chunky five-eight and wore glasses so thick it was a wonder he could see. His long hair was in a man-bun at the top of his head and his pencil stuck haphazardly out of it. "Guys, we're responsible for the first category and we've made good progress. We're through the first four codes."

"Yeah, only ten more to go," laughed Shane, the comedian of the group. He could always be counted on to lighten the mood.

"Look, we agreed to get through the first seven tonight. That leaves seven for tomorrow. We'll be able to practice our presentation on Thursday in time to present on Friday."

"Let's take a break," stated Rick. "I need to piss." He dropped his pencil on the table and stood.

Pete nodded. "Good idea. We'll start in on Bile and Liver Therapy at one-forty-five."

As everyone sat down after the break, Sue, the last member of their group and the youngest at twenty-one, grinned and said, "I've got a treat for everyone and I thought we'd play a quick game of Russian Roulette to give us some energy. We'll fly through the last three categories." She pulled a brown rectangular box from her backpack. Opening it, she tipped the box over and individual packets of Skittles, Starburst gummies, and M&Ms dropped onto the table they were all sitting around, a splash of color on a sea of gray.

Everyone perked up as they stared at the candy.

Rick asked the obvious question. "How did you get this in here? Food isn't allowed and our backpacks were all searched."

Sue looked at each team member with a naughty grin on her face. "I tucked it into my waistband. No one noticed." As everyone reached for it, she pulled the stash closer to herself. "I said we were going to play a version of Russian Roulette."

"Isn't that usually played with a gun and the winner is actually the loser?" joked Shane.

Sue sighed. "This candy is special, has a little kick. I ordered it online from a unique candy app that I'll tell you all about later. As I said, this candy is special." She emphasized special by wiggling her eyebrows.

Pete, who had known Sue since grade school, smiled. "They have coke in them?"

Sue nodded. "And other goodies."

"Coke? I could just drink a coke if I wanted one." Cindy was confused.

Laughing, Sue glanced at Cindy. "You are so naive. Cocaine. And we don't even have to snort it."

Cindy's eyes grew round. "I don't do drugs."

Rick elbowed her in the ribs. "Come on. It does nothing more than wake you up. You'll be wired and able to finish the work for tonight."

"Besides," continued Sue, "there's such a small amount in the candy, compared to snorting, that it will be just enough to get us all through the night."

"I'm in." Paul rubbed his hands together, grinning.

Anna's eyes lit up in anticipation. "You said other things and you mentioned Russian Roulette. What other things are in the candy and how do we play?"

"I'm glad you asked." Sue took a sip of water. "Marijuana and heroin are the other goodies in these treats. One bag is just plain candy, nothing added."

Cindy shook her head and began putting her things in her backpack. "Count me out. And I'm out of here."

Pete said, "Cindy, wait. We still have work to do."

At the door, she looked over her shoulder at Pete and the others, disappointment rippling off her in waves. "I won't be a part of this. I'll work on the anti-diarrheals and other agents in A-zero-seven and bring it with me when we get together tomorrow." She left without another word.

"Party pooper."

"Sue, Cindy grew up in a conservative household. Her dad is a pastor, for crying out loud. Leave her alone." Even though they were different in many ways, Anna always stood up for her friend. "Now, let's play."

"Okay. Everyone pick a candy. We'll all eat it at the same time. You have to dump all of it in your mouth and eat it at once. The loser is the one who gets the plain candy, and he or she has to buy breakfast for everyone at IHOP on Saturday morning."

Everyone nodded and began to reach for the candy.

"Wait," exclaimed Rick before anyone could select a bag. "With Cindy gone, there will be one extra bag. What if no one gets the straight candy?"

Shane laughed. "Then we all win and we'll still go

out for breakfast but pay our own way." Without waiting, he grabbed a bag of Skittles.

Sue picked up her phone. "This Russian Roulette will make a great video for YouTube and TikTok." She glanced at everyone in the room. "All set?" When everyone nodded, she started the video and said, "Go." The camera on her phone was facing out. She panned the room as she gobbled her candy. After swallowing, she spoke. "Hey everyone, this is a Russian Roulette candy challenge. Grab some special candy, you know where to get it." The camera began to wobble as Sue swayed from side to side. "Whoever gets the regular candy loses and takes the rest out for a meal." Her words stumbled out of her mouth, the slurring becoming more prevalent with each word. She giggled. "Whew, I feel really good." She started to sing "Puff the Magic Dragon," occasionally giggling in between the words.

Shane leaned back in his chair. "Whoa! Study may have to wait. This is strong. Yeah baby."

"Shane, have I ever told you how much I'd like to, you-know, with you?" Anna giggled. "My head feels light, like a balloon floating up, up and away." She snorted a laugh then covered her mouth. "Oooh, that made me dizzy." She turned her head toward Rick. "You don't look too good, Rick. Why are your lips blue?"

"Gonna be sick." He grabbed his stomach and fell to the ground, puking.

Sue glanced at Rick on the ground and began laughing. "Guess he can't handle the goods."

No one noticed Pete, who had stumbled to the door,

grasping the doorknob. Unable to turn the knob, he slid to the ground, landing on his butt. He rested his head on the wall next to the door as his breathing slowed.

Two minutes and twenty-six seconds later, Sue turned the camera on herself, using the same sing-song voice to add, "I'm thinking everyone won. Suzy Q out." She uploaded the video, dropped her phone, and passed out.

The video of five UCLA students getting high playing a game went viral on both social media venues and was shared across even more platforms, all including the hashtag, #RussianRouletteCandyChallenge. By three-fifteen in the morning, there were more than three hundred thousand views on Twitter.

CHAPTER TWELVE

Mali's apartment
Tuesday, January 11, 7:00 a.m.

MALI REACHED OVER to turn off the blaring alarm on her phone before realizing that she had not set it. The phone was ringing. Groaning, she picked it up and handed it to Jake before rolling back over and pulling the covers over her head. "Agent Black here."

"Oh, hi sir, it's Joe. I spoke with Kirsten last night. Pisses me off what's going on. I created an algorithm to search for those stickers. I emailed it to Hoop. It's built around a simple program. She just needs to download and open it on any device, select the sticker she wants to search and the desired timeframe, then press Go. The program will run in the background. I also added an open field if she wants to enter a new parameter. When the search concludes, you'll get an alert. This is the same algorithm we used for #HuntedLives and #JusticePrevails. It searches all the usual social media venues, and I added SnapChat, TikTok, and Facebook Messenger since they are the three most prevalent means of conducting illegal drug activities. I also included all of the data that we saved at the time. Each result is a link for more details."

Jake had pushed the covers back and was sitting on the side of the bed by the time Joe finished talking. "Appreciate the effort, Joe, thank you."

"Contact me if you need anything else."

"Thanks, but just work on the new case Agent Hernandez gives you." The call ended and he turned to swat Mali on her rear end. "I never knew Joe was telepathic."

"Hmmmmm?"

"Yeah, how did he know to create a means of searching for results related to those stickers? I mean, that's a gift."

Mali yawned and rolled onto her back, pushing the covers down far enough to peer at him. "Very funny." She yawned again, stretching her arms above her head. "You said not to give any details, but Kirsten knows us and there's no way she'd believe that we would sit at home and twiddle our thumbs. She offered to help. I accepted. Technically, the team hasn't been reassigned to another case yet. I told her to find out what they could before they meet with Hernandez." She grinned. "And since we're talking about this, she said she'd ask Felix if he remembers what that first sticker represents."

Jake rolled his eyes. "Anything else I should know?"

"Nope." She sat up and kissed him. "So, what did Joe have to say?"

"He sent you a program with an algorithm to search for the stickers."

"That's great. He rocks that computer." Her stomach growled and she laughed. "I'm hungry." She hopped up and went into the bathroom for a quick shower.

Fifteen minutes later, she was in the kitchen making breakfast.

"That bacon smells delicious."

"Good timing." She kissed him then handed him a cup of coffee. "Breakfast is ready."

They both sat on the stools at the island, shoveling their eggs, bacon, and wheat toast down so they could get to work. Deciding that they needed more supplies, Jake left to shop while Mali cleaned up then sat down to work.

Opening the email from Joe, she noticed that he sent individual images of the three stickers found on the box as well as the program. She downloaded the images first, displaying them on the television. All three stickers were round — the first had three heart-shaped lollipops, two were yellow and one was orange, all crossed at the bottom and fanning out at the top. A rocket was in the second sticker. And two parallel lines plus an odd-shaped sort of circle were in the third. The parallel lines went straight up two-thirds of the way then angled to the right, almost looking like a lower-case 'r'.

Downloading the program next, she marveled at how fast Joe created it and how easy it was to use. She discovered five search selections, each next to a radio button. The first three were the stickers, the fourth was an open field, and the last was All. Deciding to run a search on all three stickers for the past month, she selected All then clicked Go.

Studying the questions on the white board, Mali decided to lay out the timing of every event on a piece of paper, creating a flow chart of sorts. Visuals usually helped her. A few minutes later, as she studied the timeline, a lightbulb flashed on. Jerry got the phone call and the box arrived at the house when they were on their honeymoon. The only out-of-the-ordinary activity at the time was their honeymoon in Cabo. Someone must have recognized Jake while they were there. And the call to Jerry, as well as the box of chocolate, most likely originated from there.

Picking up her phone, she made a quick call to Jake asking for the password to the AT&T landline account. Hanging up, she logged into the account and searched the calls received starting with their wedding day. There were local calls, presumably from Jerry's friends. She recognized Paul's number but they'd have to check the other local numbers. She recognized the call they made on the fourth to say hello to Jerry and Heather. When she recognized the number that was received on the sixth, Mali froze. It started with five-two-six-two-four. That was the international code for Mexico and area code for Cabo San Lucas. But it was the remaining numbers that sent chills down her spine.

Going to her email, she scrolled down until she found the email from the Grand Solmar. They had left in such a hurry that she had asked the front desk to just email the receipt to her. Opening the document, she moved down the list of expenses, stopping in shock when she found the same number with a charge of fourteen dollars and change next to it.

She was still processing what she had learned when Jake walked in carrying a long box and two large white boards. "We need much larger boards. These will be on stands that we can roll around. I still have more bags in the car." He stopped when he got to the sofa and saw the look on Mali's face. Setting the items on the floor, he walked over to her, glancing at the images on the television as he sat down.

"What did you find?"

Mali was breathing hard. "The call to your dad was made from our suite in Cabo!"

Jake looked down at her laptop as she pointed out both numbers. "Shit." He rubbed his jaw. "Okay, so someone recognized me when we were on our honeymoon. It could be anyone and he's probably long gone at this point."

"This creeps me out. Someone was in our suite!" She rubbed the back of her neck. "Maybe the resort has a log of who entered our suite. They may also have video footage around the resort. There were numerous cameras in the public areas."

"Tim may be able to hack into their system. Who knows, though, if they store the information and, if they do, how long do they keep it?"

"One thing at a time."

"I've got to call Tim." He dialed Tim's number as he walked out the door to get the remaining bags, while Mali updated the white boards. "They're on the road, should be here shortly after lunch. Tim said he'd do what he could to get the information when they stop for gas."

"Ah, so hacking is one of those skills you mentioned?"

Jake smiled. "One of them."

They were finishing up a quick lunch of New England Clam Chowder and crackers when a loud chiming made Mali jump. They both looked at the laptop.

"The search must be finished." She moved to the laptop and punched some keys on the keyboard, displaying a list of results on the television. The list was sorted by the search parameter first, the social media venue next, followed by the date. "Wow! I only searched from the first of December until today and look how long the list is." She scrolled all the way down.

"The three lollipops sticker has the most hits and SnapChat is the most used app across the boards. Interesting," noted Jake. "Let's delve into the three lollipops first."

Mali clicked the link of the first result. Data extrapolated from the social media venue displayed.

"Whoa, this is amazing! How did Joe do that?" asked Mali as she read the comments.

They continued moving down the list, clicking each result to view the data. Most comments were just a bunch of emojis but a few comments caught Mali's eye.

"Jake, look at these comments on December twentieth. Someone is asking how to place an order for candy. One answer says the fastest way is to order from an app called Dandy Candy, then it shows a picture of the three lollipops. Another comment refers to the same app saying it's the new and best way to get your candy fast."

"Christ. Are you telling me that people are ordering drugs from a candy app that anyone can download?"

"It's possible. Or it could just be regular candy." Moving her cursor, she opened the app store and typed in *dandy candy*. Two results displayed but the first was for the Dandy Candy app. The description touted the ability to order any kind of candy in the world and receive it faster than SnapChat.

"I don't believe it!" Jake stared at the screen in disbelief. Before he could react further, his phone rang. He answered then headed to the door, saying "They're here" over his shoulder. He buzzed them in using the console on the wall next to the front door, ended the call, and opened the door to wait for them.

Mali joined Jake at the door as two men approached. One man carried two large black military-style duffel bags. The shorter man carried two black plastic bins, each secured with a bright yellow lid.

"Hey, Pirate, good to see you, amigo." The first man set his bins on the floor and wrapped Jake in a bear hug.

Jake clapped him on the back. "You too, Matey." He pulled back from him, eyes wide. "What the hell is this?" He flicked a finger at the man-bun on top of his head.

Matey grinned. "I let it grow the day I punched out. Haven't cut it since."

"Looks like a hippy, if you ask me," said the burly man standing next to him. "Skinny like 'em, too." He gently placed his bags next to the bins.

"I had no idea hippies were skinny," said Jake, ribbing the other man. "It's been too long, Sword."

"Shit, Pirate, I never thought I'd set eyes on you again." They chest bumped, much to Mali's amusement. "I'm sorry about your dad."

"Same here," said Matey.

Jake closed the door. "Thank you. I appreciate that. Let me introduce you to my wife. Mali, this is Tim Jackson, otherwise known as Matey, the best techie around." He turned to his other friend. "And this is Ben Williams, weapons specialist among other things."

"Just call me Sword, ma'am, everyone does."

"Only if you call me, Mali." She smiled and shook both men's hands. "It's a pleasure to meet you both. Come in and make yourselves comfortable."

Matey whistled as he looked around. "Nice place you have. Where can we set our stuff and where should I set up my equipment?"

"Put the bags in the corner over there," Jake said, pointing to an area to the right of the door. "And set up your equipment on the dining table next to my laptop."

Sword left to pick up two remaining bags, while Matey removed equipment from the bins and began to set up.

An hour later, Matey's computer and three monitors covered over half the dining table. The monitors were on and the computer was humming. Sword had opted to leave his equipment in the bag, unzipping one of them. They were sitting at the island eating soup and sandwiches that Mali had prepared.

"So, you think Los Rinches ordered the hit?" asked Sword in between bites.

"I'm sure of it. We found out this morning that someone recognized me in Cabo. The call to dad came from our suite."

"Damn!" exclaimed Matey. "Who called him?"

"We don't know," said Mali. "His voice sounded just like Jake's."

Matey stopped mid-chew. Swallowing, he asked, "Do you have the recording?"

Jake nodded.

"Shit, why didn't you tell me sooner?" He dropped the remainder of his sandwich onto the plate and swung about to face the dining table. In one step, he was at his computer punching in keys. "I developed a program that can filter out fake accents and other elements of speech to get to the true voice, needed it for a job in Germany a few years back. A voice specialist helped me with the parameters." He turned his head to look at Mali and Jake. "Hello? The recording?"

Jake grinned. "Ah, it's good to be working with you again, Matey." He glanced at Mali. "You'll find that Matey is like a dog with a bone when it comes to work."

Mali walked over to her laptop, picked up the flash drive that was sitting next to it, and handed it to Matey's outstretched hand.

Sword, who had finished his meal, looked at the television for the first time. "What's that list of?"

"It's the results of a search. The techie on my team developed the program this morning. It allows us to search for pretty much anything on the most-used social media venues."

Matey looked up from his computer. "No kidding! Show it to me."

"He also loses focus just as fast," said Sword, cuffing him on the shoulder.

"Hey, the program's churning on its own. It won't go any faster with me staring at it." Matey smacked Sword on the back of his head as he passed him to stand behind the sofa and study the boards and the television. Sword joined him.

Mali sat in front of her laptop and ran another search, this time entering #HuntedLives in the open field with the date parameters set to the time when they were dealing with the game.

"#HuntedLives?" asked Sword.

"A case we worked on a few months ago. That's when Hoop and I met."

"Hoop?"

Mali grinned. "You're not the only ones with a nickname. My maiden name is Hooper. I have no idea who started it but it has stuck."

Ding, ding, ding.

Turning her eyes back to the laptop, she displayed the results.

"As you can see, the venue most used was Twitter. When you click on any result, more details are provided." She demonstrated how it worked.

"Damn good programming," said Matey, admiration in his voice. "Send the program to me, I'd like to take a closer look."

Sword was staring at the details of one result Mali had clicked. "That case looked pretty bad."

Mali's smile dropped as she, too, reviewed the details. She had inadvertently clicked on the day the woman in San Antonio was killed on the Riverwalk.

"The comments were brutal." Jake, too, was staring at the television. He shook his head. "People often say and do things out of the bounds of morality when anonymous." Everyone was quiet for a few moments. "We have a lot to do, let's get to it."

Sword nodded then walked to his open bag, picking up a bug detector. He walked through the apartment, eyes focused on the handheld device. "I'm going to check for bugs every day."

Jake chuckled. "Some things never change."

"It pays to be diligent," was his only response.

Matey returned his computer. "Oh, I forgot to tell you that I have that information from the resort in Cabo you asked for."

"Video recordings?" asked Jake.

Matey nodded. "They keep recordings for thirty days. I grabbed everything they had from the first until the time you left. Want me to pull them up?"

"No, put them on a flash drive. Hoop and I can put them on our devices and begin going through them."

"You got it." A few minutes later, he handed the drive to Jake who downloaded the files onto his laptop then tossed it to Mali, who did the same.

Looking at the files, Mali sighed. "This will take a while. There are recordings from the lobby covering the registration desk and main room, from the lobby looking out toward the entrance, and from the pool area."

"What are these text files and images?" asked Jake.

"What? Oh, phone records from your suite as well as the front desk, employee records including their pictures, logged entries into your suite, that sort of thing."

"Great work, Matey."

"Hoop, I'll start with the text files then I'll move to the videos of the pool area. You take the lobby and entry."

Mali nodded. Before she could start, her phone rang.

"Hoop, it's Felix. I have some info for you."

"Hi Felix. You're not calling from the office, right? I don't want you to get into trouble."

"No, I had to leave early for a dentist appointment. It's been crazy at the cavern this morning, by the way. Our new case is a boring tracking case using the ghosts. Jeff and Joe are working while the rest of us are twiddling our thumbs. At least for now," he whined.

Mali ignored what he said. "What do you have for us?"

"Oh, I remembered where I saw the three lollipops. They are the logo for a candy app."

"We discovered that this morning."

"But it's different. The logo on the box your dad received has two yellow lollipops and one orange one. The official logo has three yellow lollipops. I've ordered candy from this app before and it always has three yellow lollipops. Another thing, the second sticker on my orders has always been blank."

"This helps, Felix. Thanks."

"Sure thing. Wish me luck in surviving the next two weeks."

He sounded so forlorn, Mali was chuckling as she hung up.

She passed on the information from Felix and told Jake that she was going to follow up on the orange heart and rocket before reviewing the videos.

Opening Google in her browser, she searched *orange heart emoji*. The results only mentioned warmth, care, and sunshine. It was nothing out of the ordinary. The same type of results displayed for *rocket emoji*. It was used to signify success and ambition. She changed her search to *orange heart and rocket emojis* then *orange heart emoji code*, and *rocket emoji code*, but nothing new displayed.

Mali took a deep breath and looked up from her screen. Glancing at the white board with the cartel-related questions, her eyes narrowed as she considered everything she had learned. Looking back at her screen, she modified the search to *drugs and orange heart emoji code*.

"Whoa!" The list of results was extensive. She clicked the first link, from the DEA. "Oh my God! Jake, you've got to see this." She put the graphic on the television screen. "Kids are using emojis in code to buy drugs."

CHAPTER THIRTEEN

EVERYONE STOPPED WHAT they were doing to look at the screen.

Jake walked over to stand behind Mali. "Jesus," said Jake. "Ordering drugs using emojis as code? Unbelievable."

Sword, back at the table after finishing his sweep, was shaking his head. "Wow! Kids can sure be devious these days."

"They've always been devious, Sword, it's just a little easier with all the social media," returned Matey.

Studying the list, Jake said, "There are codes for oxycodone and xanax, cocaine, marijuana, meth, and even codes for potency. A blue heart is code for meth, an orange heart is fentanyl, a rocket means…" His eyes shot to Mali's as comprehension dawned.

Mali's eyebrows shot up and her eyes were wide. "Oh my God." She placed the image of the three stickers from the order Jerry received back on the television screen.

"Shit," said Matey, shaking his head in disbelief.

Sword looked stunned.

Jake crossed his arms over his chest, his lips were pinched together in a thin line. "A rocket represents high potency. The box dad received was an order for chocolate with a high potency of fentanyl."

No one said a word as they absorbed the implications.

"Jake, I feel my time would be better spent researching this. I also recall hearing a news report about a young teen who died from fentanyl-laced candy. There may be others. I want to confirm whether or not they got their candy from the same candy app, plus I want to research the app itself, find out where it's based."

Jake didn't respond.

"Jake?"

He blinked a few times before glancing at Mali. "Good idea."

Sword walked over to his bag, reached in and grabbed a few items before returning to the others. He handed a burner phone to Matey at the table before walking over to Mali and Jake. After giving her a phone, he passed the last one to Jake then handed him a gun with an accompanying holster. "I assumed the FBI took your weapon when they put you on leave."

Jake pocketed the burner phone, placed the holster on the back of the sofa, and turned the gun over in his hand. "A Sig Sauer semi-auto. Nice. What are the burners for?"

"Use these phones from now on. Each one is programmed with all of the others. Turn your phones off, and give your burner numbers only to those who absolutely need it. It pays to be diligent."

"Smart." He knuckle-punched Sword on his shoulder. "I want you to go through the text files and images. I'll take all the videos."

"What am I looking for?"

"Anything out of the ordinary."

Mali's phone rang. It was her mother. Shrugging, she told Sword she had to take it. "I'll call her right back with my burner phone." Standing, she looked at Jake. "This is a good opportunity for us to talk to Heather."

He nodded and they both walked outside onto the balcony.

"Hello Mother. How are you? And how is Heather?"

"Jasmine, darling. We are all fine. Heather is learning how to play the piano. I know she'll want to tell you all about it."

Mali smiled. "I need to call you right back, okay?"

"Well, of course. I'll be here all afternoon."

"Thanks." Mali hung up, set down her phone, and picked up the burner phone. When her mother answered, Mali said, "You're on speaker phone and Jake is here. Is Father with you?"

"He's golfing at the club today. Hello Jacob. I almost didn't answer the phone. It says Unknown Caller on my screen."

"This is a temporary phone I'll be using for a while. Let me give you the number."

Willow repeated it back to her. "What's going on?"

"It's good to hear your voice, Willow," replied Jake.

"We'll explain everything to you and Charles later this evening, if that's all right."

"Of course it is. I have to say, though, that my worst fears of you joining the FBI have come to fruition, Jasmine. All this subterfuge, the game a few months ago, your father's business partner, not to mention the added security here." She sighed.

"Mother…"

"I know I'm preaching to the choir, but we're concerned for all of you."

"We appreciate that, Willow," said Jake, "which is why we are exercising an abundance of caution."

"Mother, can we speak to Heather?"

Willow sighed again. "She's in her Zoom class right now. Why don't I have her call you after dinner, say seven o'clock? Then we can talk afterward."

"That works. Thank you, Mother, for everything."

"Take care of our daughter, Jacob."

Mali rolled her eyes, making Jake smile.

"You've got my word on that."

After they hung up, Jake picked up Mali's hand and squeezed it. "They're not going to like what I have to tell them."

Mali frowned. "What are you going to say?"

"Added security isn't going to be enough. Your parents need to take a vacation with Heather, disappear for a while."

Mali stared into his eyes and read the concern. "If they could find out where you lived, then they can also find my parents' house." He nodded. "What about my sisters and their families?"

"I believe they'll be okay. He's only interested in Heather."

"Do we need to move our operation from here? Won't they find this apartment?"

Jake nodded. "We move today." He stood and pulled her up with him. "I want to talk with Sword and Matey about this."

They walked back into the living room.

"I've got the original voice from the recording. It's ninety-seven percent accurate, according to my program."

"Let's hear it."

They all gathered next to Matey's computer to listen.

"Definitely Hispanic but I don't recognize it," said Jake.

"I sent the recording to Carson. Hopefully, he can put a name to the voice."

Jake nodded. "Good. In the meantime, we're moving. If they found my house, they'll eventually find this place."

Matey and Sword both nodded. "And your daughter?"

"She's with Mali's parents. We're going to tell them to disappear for a while."

Mali mumbled, "I hate to break everything down when we're just beginning to make progress."

"Matey, look for a home in a remote location, somewhere well outside of the City toward Scranton. You know what we need. Get a short-term rental, we'll pay cash for it."

"On it." He turned back to his computer to begin his search.

"I'll pack up everything but Matey's computer and primary monitor," said Sword.

"I'll help," said Jake. "What type of vehicle did you rent?"

"A suburban. We wanted a lot of room."

"Good. Since you can carry everything, I'll rent something small and fast."

"You think someone's watching us?"

"So soon? Doubtful. But I'd rather not take any chances on someone recognizing our vehicles."

"Got it," called out Matey. "It's remote, a few miles outside of Covington and twenty minutes from Scranton." He turned the monitor for Jake to scan.

"Looks good. Book it. I want you and Sword to head there now. Pay in cash and start to set things up."

Fifteen minutes later, they walked out the door with the final load of equipment. Jake went with them to help, carrying a box of breakfast food so they wouldn't have to shop for groceries until tomorrow.

Mali walked into the bedroom to pack their clothes and toiletries. Looking around, she could only chuckle at the disaster. They had not fully unpacked from their honeymoon. Clothes were strewn across the bed and a pile of dirty clothes sat in a corner.

* * *

5:20 p.m.

Jake and Mali were almost ready to leave for Covington when the doorbell rang. Alarmed, Jake pulled the gun out of its holster and quietly took a position next to the door. He motioned for her to stay in the kitchen. Peeking around the wall, Mali watched Jake.

"Who is it?"

"Jake, it's me, Kirsten."

Jake took a deep breath, relaxed and holstered his gun.

Mali was walking toward the door when Jake opened it, ushering Kirsten inside.

She smiled at Jake and hugged Mali. Noticing their bags and a large cooler on the floor behind Mali, she asked, "Where are you going and how can I help?"

Jake said, "The less you know, the better."

"I'm serious. I want to help. Hernandez has us on a bullshit assignment. I think they're going to split us up. The only good thing is that she put Jeff in charge. I was afraid she was going to stay with us. I left early saying I was sick."

Mali sighed. "Not a good idea, Kirsten. We don't know what we're getting into or how long this will take. Our jobs are already at risk. You could lose your job."

Kirsten placed her hands on Mali's shoulders and stared into her eyes. "We've been friends for a long time now, and friends stick together. If I lose this job, I'll get another. I've got badass computer skills, after all." She smiled.

"What about Jen? And we're leaving right now, by the way. What about clothes and stuff?" asked Jake.

"I can go home and pack, won't be far behind you. Jen will understand."

Mali looked at Jake, who was considering Kirsten's words.

"Go home and pack enough clothes for four or five days. Call Hernandez on your phone saying you're worse than you thought and will be out for a few days. Then leave your phone at home. Don't tell Jen, or anyone, where you're going. Take Hoop's burner phone." Mali reached into her bag and handed her the phone. "You'll get your own burner when you join us and you can pass that number on to Jen, if you must, but my preference is that you don't. Head west out of the City toward New Jersey. We'll text you the address when you're on the road."

Kirsten grinned from ear to ear. "I won't let you down. See you soon."

"Is it wise to involve her?" asked Mali after Jake had closed the door.

"We can use her skills and we need another set of hands." He reached behind her to grab the bags. "Let's head out. According to GPS, it's going to take us an hour and a half to get to the house."

* * *

Remote house, 8 miles west of Covington, PA
Wednesday, January 12, 8:30 a.m.

Jake and Mali had arrived at the four-bedroom farmhouse the previous evening. They had called Willow and Charles when they stopped for dinner in a little town outside Newark. Willow and Charles were actually happy to leave, saying they hadn't been on vacation in ages. Willow wanted to go someplace warm and with sand, and Charles said that as long as a golf course was nearby, he'd be happy. They agreed not to tell anyone where they were going. Heather was excited when Jake and Mali told her that she was going on a vacation with Papa and Grammy, but she wished her mommy and daddy could join them. They promised her that they would be with her soon.

The house sat on ten acres and included a large barn with an attached shed. By the time they had arrived, the televisions in the bedrooms had been brought to the main room, an open-concept space with a large living room, dining room, and kitchen. The living room had a vaulted ceiling with three wood beams running the length of the room. Sofas and chairs surrounded the stone fireplace. A wooden rectangular dining table separated the living room from the kitchen. Mali was charmed by the rustic look and feel of the home and property.

Above the mantle was a seventy-five-inch television. The forty-six-inch televisions from the bedrooms were placed on tables next to the fireplace, two on each side.

Kirsten helped Matey link all five televisions together, tying them to Matey's computer which sat on the dining table along with the printer, and Jake and Kirsten's laptops. Mali's station was at one end of the kitchen island. She had transferred the questions from the small white boards to the two larger ones that Jake had purchased, and had updated them. Both were positioned on the right side of the room. Sword's tools, Matey called them his toys, including the bug detector and a 3D printer with ink and supplies, were positioned at the other end of the island. The larger weapons and extra burner phones remained in his other duffel bag, which was sitting on the floor under the dining table.

"So, why do you need a 3D printer?" Kirsten asked Sword, stepping up to inspect it.

"I make small weapons with it. They are undetectable and often come in handy."

"You think we'll need them?"

"It pays to be diligent."

Just before breakfast, Mali's phone rang.

"Jasmine, we're on our way, won't say where."

"Thank you for letting us know, Father."

"We didn't want you to worry. The security detail I hired is going with us, by the way, and I deposited some money in your account just in case you need it."

Mali's eyebrows shot up. "Thank you. I appreciate that. It might come in handy."

"Take care and find the bastards who killed Jerry."

Breakfast was finished and the dishes were cleaned and put away, when Jake called everyone together.

"Before we get started, I just want to thank all of you, again, for your help. We couldn't do this without it, and I wasn't about to leave dad's murder to the DEA to solve. They have much bigger fish to fry." He looked at each member of the new team. "A few rules…Covington is a small town. I don't want anyone to go there for any reason. We'd stick out like a sore thumb. Scranton is only twenty minutes away. If we need anything, we'll travel there. If anyone enquires, we are in the entertainment industry working a new project." Everyone nodded. "Mali listed the main research tasks we need to tackle on the white board." Mali walked over to the board and picked up a red marker, updating the board as Jake spoke. "I'll take all videos from the resort, Sword will review the text files and images. Hoop, look into those other drug-related deaths you mentioned and find out what you can about the candy app. Matey, follow up with Carson and try to put a name to that voice. Then I want you and Kirsten to figure out how the candy app works. How does someone order regular candy versus candy with drugs?"

"I'll download the candy app and get started while Matey contacts Carson," said Kirsten.

"If you find something, say something. Any information could change our trajectory. Any questions?" No one said anything. "Good, let's get started."

Mali set the marker down and returned to her laptop. Navigating to the website of her favorite television station, WABC, she began searching previous news reports. She flipped through articles starting on December first and working her way forward. She stopped when she recognized an article about a teen death from fentanyl-laced candy. It was dated December twentieth.

She had just clicked the link to read the article when Matey hung up his phone and said, "I just spoke to Carson. He told me that the voice belongs to a man they call Cenzo. He's been with Los Rinches for about eight years now. He can imitate any voice, and rapidly moved up in the ranks of the cartel because of that skill. He's a gringo, real name is Matt Spencer. Here's the most recent picture they have of him." Matey displayed a picture. Mali had continued to read the article while Matey spoke, listening with half an ear, but looked up to view the picture.

"Good grief, he looks like he could be a surfer with that blond hair and tan body," said Kirsten.

"Make no mistake," said Matey. "According to Carson, he is said to be as brutal as Armano when it comes to killing. He's been on their radar for a couple of years. The Army hasn't been able to capture him or take him out, he's as wily as Armano. They evidently change locations every couple of days." Matey looked at Jake. "He was one of the survivors from our raid."

Jake's eyes shot to Matey then returned to the screen. "Damn it. Was he in Cabo because of me?"

"Carson doesn't seem to think so."

"Hmmmm…well, at least we know who we're looking for in the videos and other files. Thanks, Matey."

"Jake, I found an article on a teen who died in Brooklyn on December twentieth of a fentanyl overdose.

I remember reading about it at the time. He was eating gummy bears and it was reported a few days later that the candy was laced with fentanyl." She paused to sip her Diet Coke. "And get this, he ordered the candy online without his mother's knowledge. While the report doesn't say how he placed the order, a box with no return address was found with the candy. No pictures, everything was confiscated by the DEA." Still looking at her monitor and scanning other articles, her shoulders slumped and her hand covered her mouth. "Oh no," she whispered. Swallowing, she raised her head to look at everyone. "On the twenty-eighth, nine boys overdosed on fentanyl-laced lollipops while at a birthday party. There were no survivors. The mother of the birthday boy ordered the candy from a candy app and told officers that she had used it in the past. She added that she was late ordering the candy and rushed through the process. She wanted to make sure it arrived on time."

"How horrible!" exclaimed Kirsten, tearing up.

"Jake, they were just a couple years older than Heather. How could anyone do that?"

"More importantly, how did the mother get tainted candy when she's used the app before? I have a hard time believing she did it intentionally." He squeezed her shoulder. "I'd be willing to bet that all orders were placed using the candy app."

Kirsten said, "The DEA has no doubt confiscated everything from these cases. We're kind of stuck without seeing pictures of all the boxes and reading the reports."

Matey smiled. "I may be able to help in that department."

Everyone turned to stare at him.

"Don't tell me you can hack into the DEA," said Jake, frowning.

"Let's just say that the government agency we do contract work for has needed info from the DEA and, most of the time, they are not forthcoming with information. They do not like to play in the sandbox. I found one of the backdoors into their network and have tapped into it from time to time. Don't worry, any activity on my end just sounds like white noise to them."

Jake rubbed the back of his neck. "Christ, Matey, what agency did you say you work for?"

"I didn't." He grinned. "Do you want me to take a look?"

Jake pinched the bridge of his nose before taking a deep breath. "We found all of the information fairly easily. You can bet that the DEA already knows about Dandy Candy, perhaps more as well." He studied Matey then each team member. "Hell, we've already started down the rabbit hole, we might as well go all the way. Pass on whatever you find to Hoop, then get back to the app. We need to know how it works, now more than ever."

CHAPTER FOURTEEN

Mali placed her headphones over her ears and listened to WABC, without disturbing the others, while she began researching Dandy Candy. She wasn't waiting for Matey. She didn't know how long it would take him or what information he would be able to provide. Since she only had her laptop, and was not set up with two monitors, she displayed the WABC livestream in a small window in the lower corner of her screen and opened a larger window for her research.

There was a buzz of activity as everyone focused on their tasks.

"Breaking news," began the reporter on WABC. Mali's eyes dropped to the small window. "We have just learned that five college students attending UCLA in California have overdosed on candy spiked with drugs. They were studying at a library when they decided to play a game they called the Russian Roulette Candy Challenge in the early morning hours. One of the students videotaped the event, which has gone viral on social media. We have the video and have decided to broadcast it, with the faces of the students blurred to protect their privacy. This station realizes how serious the opioid crisis is and we feel that showing the realities of it is crucial to increase awareness and, hopefully, to galvanize the public into taking action to eliminate this crisis. We warn you that the video is graphic and hard to watch."

A few seconds later, the video began. Mali's blood chilled as she watched it.

When it ended, the reporter continued. "Some students who saw the video as it live-streamed contacted the police. It took them awhile to locate the library on campus where they were studying and then the room they were in. Two students were pronounced dead at the scene, the other three were taken to the hospital in critical condition. The video issued a Russian Roulette Candy Challenge for other students. We strongly encourage all students to ignore this challenge and to stay safe. We will update you when we have more information. Now to Gina and the weather. Gina?"

"Oh my God!" Mali was shaking her head, one hand rubbing her stomach. She thought she might be sick.

She didn't realize how loud she was talking since she was wearing the headphones.

"What's up?" asked Kirsten.

"What?" Mali removed the headphones. "Oh, I'm listening to a report on WABC about five college kids in California who overdosed on candy and issued a challenge for others to do the same." She shook her head as the others approached her at the kitchen island. "The challenge is to choose candy, some of which is laced with drugs, and eat it. The loser is the one who eats plain candy and doesn't get high. But as the reporter stated, they all overdosed and two died because all the candy was spiked." She played the video again. "They'll run tests to determine what drugs they consumed."

"Jesus," exclaimed Sword.

"She's talking about getting special candy. Is she referring to Dandy Candy?" asked Kirsten.

Jake's eyes narrowed. "Play it again and look at what's on the table." As Mali started the video again, he pointed to the screen. "There! Stop the video." Everyone studied the screen. "Isn't that a plain box next to the last bag of candy?"

"Could be," said Sword, angling his head and trying to see it better.

Matey's computer chimed. He stepped to it, punched a few keys on the keyboard, then pulled a flash drive out of his computer, turning to hand it to Mali. "I searched for anything related to Dandy Candy and candy laced with fentanyl. I limited the search to the past two months. I was able to grab more than pictures, didn't look at the details though."

"Perfect. Thanks."

"I found the Twitter feed for the challenge game. Here's the link, Matey," said Kirsten.

Matey opened the link for #RussianRouletteCandyChallenge on one of the smaller televisions.

The video displayed first followed by countless comments.

"RAD game!"

"Looks like fun."

"My friends and I are going to play, I already ordered the candy, should be here tomorrow."

"Seems kind of dangerous."

"Did she say what drugs were in the candy?"

"I want to play."

The comments went on and on, and there were more than a half million views of the video.

"My God! How can they think it would be a fun game?" asked Mali.

"Kirsten," began Jake.

"I'm contacting Twitter right now. I'll also call You-Tube, and it goes without saying that everything is being saved as we speak," said Kirsten, interrupting Jake.

"Thanks. We need all of it removed as fast as possible."

Sword was frowning. "Once it's out there, it's there forever. Who knows how many social media apps this is playing on."

Jake turned on Sword, scowling. "You're right, it's everywhere and this likely won't make an impact. But, dammit, we have to try. Every little thing we do adds up." He was breathing in short, rapid breaths.

Sword put both hands up in a conciliatory gesture, backing up a step or two.

"Sword, when we were dealing with the Hunted Lives game and Janet's sick game after, we removed what we could from social media whenever we found it." Mali spoke quietly. "Did it make a difference? At the very least, it slowed things down and minimized the number of people who saw it."

Jake looked at Matey. "Get the IP address for every user that specifically says they've ordered candy and/or plan to play the game. We need to identify them and stop them from playing."

"Can do, Pirate, but it's going to take some time. Don't you want Kirsten and I to figure out how the candy app works? Can't do both."

Jake rubbed the back of his neck and sighed. "You're right. The authorities will have to handle the challenge. Get started on the app."

Sword, Matey, and Kirsten returned to their stations.

Jake took a deep breath. "There's too much to do."

"We can't do everything. If we're going to find Armano, we need to stay on task."

Jake swallowed and looked away. "He placed a simple order from Dandy Candy, killed dad without leaving his house, or wherever he's holed up."

"Then we expose Dandy Candy for what it is and close it down."

Jake smiled as he turned his gaze to her. "I love your optimism." He studied the group. "We need more people."

Mali squeezed his hand before returning to the files from the DEA that Matey had given her.

Shortly before four, Matey and Kirsten said they knew how the people ordered drugs.

"We don't have every detail from the code but we have enough info to show you," explained Kirsten.

Matey opened the Dandy Candy app on the large television and signed in. "Notice how the logo has three yellow heart lollipops?"

"As Felix told me," said Mali.

Matey nodded. "When I place a regular order…" he added some candy to his cart, "the candy is clean." He finished placing the order. "The lollipops on the logo remain yellow throughout the entire order."

"This is the fourth order we've placed and they're all going to Felix's house, by the way," said Kirsten.

Jake's eyebrows shot up.

Kirsten held up her hand. "Before you say anything, I called Felix on my new burner phone while he was at lunch. I knew he'd be out of the office. He always goes to lunch at the same time. He's bored. He said we could send stuff to his apartment. He'll keep it for us until we need it. Quite honestly, I think he'd join us if you asked."

"I'll consider it, but it's going to look suspicious if team members continue to leave one by one." He took a deep breath. "Continue with the app."

"We discovered in the code that if you click the logo four times rapidly, the screen reloads and you can order spiked candy." Matey clicked the logo four times. "Look at what happens when I select a candy." He selected gummy bears. The details that displayed included six emojis beneath the quantity selection. "As you know, the snowflake is cocaine, blue heart is meth, brown heart is heroin, red heart is MDMA, and the orange heart beneath the four emojis is fentanyl." He moved the cursor over each emoji as he spoke. "The user can order any of the four drugs and if they want it laced with fentanyl, they can also click the orange heart. They can select the rocket that's next to the orange heart if they also want high potency."

Mali's mouth dropped open. "Oh my God!"

"Okay, the logo on the box identifies if the candy is straight or spiked. And if they select the rocket, the drugs will be high potency," said Jake.

Kirsten nodded. "That's right."

"Because there were two yellow lollipops and one orange one on dad's box of chocolate, the candy was only laced with fentanyl. But the rocket indicates that the chocolate had high levels of fentanyl in it."

The room was quiet as they absorbed the information.

Sword finally asked, "What happens if someone orders candy with all of the drugs? There are only three lollipops. And what if some candy is ordered with high potency and others are not? How does the user know?"

"We don't have answers to that yet," said Matey. "But we did place an order with that exact scenario. We can verify for ourselves when the boxes arrive."

"Actually, I can answer that question," said Mali. "The info from the DEA clarifies some of this."

She returned to her laptop, moved some files into a new folder she created on the flash drive, then ejected the drive and handed it to Matey. "Open the four images, one on each of the small televisions."

Matey did as asked and four boxes appeared.

"The first box is from the young teen who ordered all that candy. Zoom in on the stickers, the clarity is excellent."

Everyone studied the image.

"On the logo, the first lollipop is yellow, but the other two indicate that his order included candy with marijuana and fentanyl. The candy was high potency given that the second sticker had the rocket."

"Does the yellow lollipop mean that some of the candy is straight?" asked Kirsten.

Matey shook his head. "No, when you click the logo four times to order drugged candy, that's all you can order. You can't mix them."

Mali continued. "Now look at the picture on the TV below the image we just reviewed. It's an order form that was inside the box, as noted by the DEA's handwritten message that's next to it. It itemizes each candy and indicates what's in it and whether or not it's high potency."

"Wait a minute," said Jake. "You didn't find an order form with dad's box, right?"

Mali looked surprised. "You're right. I didn't." Her eyes narrowed in concern. "So where is it? Or better yet, why wasn't there an order form?"

No one had the answer.

Shaking her head to clear her thoughts, Mali said, "If you look at the third image on the top right, it's the box from the order that the mom placed for her nine-year-old son's birthday party. The order form is below it. As you'll see, the lollipops she ordered had high levels of fentanyl. She said she had ordered from the app before without any problems."

Sword said, "I'm no expert at using computers but I've placed orders on Amazon before. And I have to tell you, I'm not a patient man. If my internet is slow, I've been known to click the same key multiple times. When you click the logo on any app, isn't it supposed to take you to the home page? What if her internet was slow and she clicked the logo multiple times?"

"What are the odds?" asked Jake. "And if it was that easy to get to the illegal part of the site, wouldn't more people be inadvertently ordering drugs?" He turned to Matey. "How long has this app been out there? Can you determine if the illegal part of the app was always there, or added later?"

"We can easily check when the app was first released. We'll have to delve into each update to identify if and when the illegal part was added."

Mali said, "Matey, put the next file on the main screen. It's an email dated two days ago, sent from the phone of Harvey Atters, a DEA agent who was looking into Dandy Candy. The email was addressed to Christine Beckons, the agent-in-charge of investigating the recent deaths related to fentanyl-laced candy and the app. He said he had information and needed to speak with her in person immediately, couldn't risk talking on an unsecure line. He wanted to meet in the Mall by the Washington monument in DC that same day."

"Interesting," said Jake.

"He never made it. Display the last file, please." She looked up at the new document. "It's an email from Beckons, sent yesterday, informing the staff that Atters was killed in a car accident. She doesn't explicitly say that the accident occurred before their meeting but she tasks two agents to find out what Atters knew."

"Christ." Jake stared at the email. "What the hell did Atters discover?"

"There's more."

Everyone turned their heads to look at Mali.

"We still don't know what the last sticker means, right? I've been looking at the documents and images Matey gave me. It's obvious that the DEA is trying to figure out who owns Dandy Candy. The app itself gives the name of a shell company that has been untraceable. They believe that the third sticker on the box is a clue as to who owns it. They're guessing, but I've been thinking about it and reviewing maps of large U.S. cities." She turned back to her laptop. A moment later, she said, "Matey, I've sent you an email with two more images. Display the first one on the big screen."

The image that appeared was a picture of the third sticker, enlarged.

"We've been looking at the two lines as just two parallel lines. What if the lines are a location, specifically, a street?"

As one, the team frowned in confusion.

Her eyes lit up. "Bear with me. We also believe that Armano is involved in some way. At a minimum, he knew about the app and ordered the chocolate from it." She paused. "What if the squiggly circle identifies who owns Dandy Candy?"

"You've totally lost me," exclaimed Kirsten.

Mali glanced at Matey. "Can you overlay the second image I created on top of the first one?"

He nodded, typed on his keyboard and when he pressed enter, the second image floated onto the screen covering the first image.

Sword's mouth dropped open. "Shit! That looks like the Strip at Las Vegas. The other one looks like a badge of some sort."

Mali nodded, staring at Jake. "I believe it's the badge for the border patrol."

His eyes widened as comprehension dawned. "Los Rinches."

"Yes. I believe Dandy Candy is based in Las Vegas and owned by Los Rinches."

CHAPTER FIFTEEN

Base of Operations, 8 miles west of Covington, PA
Thursday, January 13, 1:30 p.m.

ACCEPTING THE FACT that the team needed more help, Jake had agreed to ask Felix to join them, if he was willing to accept the possible consequences. Felix had jumped at the chance when Jake and Mali spoke with him the prior evening. The candy that Matey ordered was due to arrive at Felix's apartment later today, so Kirsten was going back to the City to pick him up. Sword was traveling with her and driving the suburban. They had agreed to meet at his apartment in Jersey City at five-thirty.

As Kirsten and Sword were preparing to leave, Matey motioned for Jake to join him.

Mali said, "I'd like to call Agent Whitby while you get an update from Matey." Angela Whitby helped Jake and the team last September when Mali's adversary, Janet Simpson, took her. Agent Whitby had helped them track Mali from the moment she landed in Vegas through the time of Janet's demise in Lake Tahoe.

"Good idea." Jake gave her Agent Whitby's number and walked over to Matey.

"Agent Whitby," a firm voice answered on the first ring.

"Angela, this is Agent Hooper. We met last—"

"Mali, it's good to hear your voice. How are you, and how is Agent Black?"

"Jake proposed shortly after our return from Tahoe. We were married twelve days ago."

"Wow! Congratulations! I could see the love between you back then. You must be over the moon."

"Mixed emotions right now. Yes, I am beyond thrilled. But we've had a tragedy in our family and need your help." Mali explained the sequence of events from their honeymoon to Jerry's death and being put on leave, to the cartel's involvement and the candy app. "It's a lot to ask, especially since we're going against orders and will probably be fired at the end of this. We now firmly believe that Dandy Candy is run by the Los Rinches cartel and their distribution center is based in Las Vegas. We're trying to figure out where."

"I've lived in Vegas all my life and know the area pretty well. Let me do some checking on my end. There are two facilities, that I am aware of, that are large enough. There's probably more. No doubt they're operating under a false name."

"The app gives the name of a shell company. Hang on." Mali flipped through some documents on her laptop, looking for the name. "The name given is Patsy's."

Angela chuckled. "That's fitting. Lollipops are sometimes called patsy's."

"You're kidding."

"Where I grew up, we called them suckers or patsy's. I preferred patsy's."

"Good Lord. I did a search earlier and couldn't find any company in Vegas called Patsy's."

"Not surprising. Give me a few hours to do my thing and I'll call you back."

"Thank you, Angela. We really appreciate it. Call back on this number, by the way. It's a burner." She gave the number to Angela.

"Will do."

They hung up as Kirsten walked over to her.

"We're heading out. Sword has an errand he wants to run. Given the traffic, we'll probably get back late."

"Thanks for going, Kirsten. Be careful."

Kirsten laughed. "I'm not worried." She pointed to Sword. "He's carrying, and even if he wasn't, no one is about to mess with him. Felix will probably shit a brick when he sees Sword."

Mali giggled, gave her a quick hug, then joined Matey and Jake at the table.

"Agent Whitby's going to help." Mali relayed the information from her phone call.

"Good. Matey discovered that the illegal aspect of the app was put in place nine months ago."

Matey added, "It's rapidly becoming the place to order drugs, and will soon overtake SnapChat in that capacity."

"Why don't the authorities just shut it down?"

"I believe that the DEA is only now tying the recent fentanyl-laced overdoses to the app," said Jake.

"I created a program that identifies orders placed on SnapChat, Facebook Messenger, and Dandy Candy. For the first two, I had to create an algorithm that takes all of the drug-related emojis and combines more than one in different orders."

Mali frowned. "In English, Matey."

"You have to look at the context of how the emojis are used. Any one of the emojis could be totally innocent and unrelated to drugs. A red heart could mean I love you when sent by itself to someone. But if you use that red heart with a crown and a cookie, you could be a drug dealer advertising that you sell large batches of MDMA."

Mali's mouth dropped open. "How can parents keep up with things like this?" She shook her head.

Matey continued. "For the Dandy Candy app, I only had to search for the emojis that were on the order form, it could be one, multiple, or all of them."

"What did you find?" asked Jake.

"The search is for the last two years. I extrapolated the data and created this chart." Their eyes shifted to the big screen. "As you can see, there is a steady rise in drug orders for SnapChat and Messenger, although the order rate for Messenger is much lower than Snap-Chat. It gets interesting when Dandy Candy goes live with the capability to place illegal orders. Things start slow as users learn how to place orders through the app.

At month four, Messenger orders begin to decline and SnapChat orders slow considerably. At the nine-month mark, orders through Dandy Candy are exceeding orders placed through SnapChat."

Jake studied the data. "When did Dandy Candy appear on the DEA's radar?"

"Hard to say," said Matey.

Mali said, "Run the program that Joe created. For the parameter, use *candy app*, and search for the same two-year time period."

A few minutes later, the computer chimed and Matey displayed the results. Starting with the most recent date and working backward, Matey clicked each result and they reviewed the details.

"The candy app isn't even mentioned until October. And no one calls it by name." Jake whistled. "So the DEA's involvement with Dandy Candy is recent. Good work. We're on the right track and might be one step ahead of them. Let's keep moving forward."

* * *

Los Angeles, CA
Thursday, January 13, 3:30 p.m.

The tent city stretched down San Vicente Boulevard in front of the West Los Angeles Veterans Administration campus. Called Veterans Row, the area was pristine compared to other homeless camps, and American flags adorned every tent. The pride displayed by the veterans, despite their circumstances, was evident. The 'city' was run like a military base, with a chain of command and a rotating list of tasks, like sweeping, picking up trash and properly disposing it, or keeping watch. Forty-plus 'residents' lived there.

On this sunny day, six veterans were sitting in the common area they had set up behind the tents. Fold up chairs were grouped around a makeshift fire pit that was actually a barrel that had been cut in half length-wise and laid on its side. They often burned appropriate trash, like cardboard and branches, to keep warm on cold evenings. Not assigned any duties this day, they were drinking water and talking about their latest efforts to get support from the VA behind them.

"I delivered all the forms this morning, got the usual bullshit response," said Carl, a grizzly ex-Marine, scruffy gray beard touching his chest. He grimaced as he looked at their appointed commander.

"Damn them." Bob Tanker took a deep drag on the cigarette pinched between his thumb and forefinger before flicking it into the fire pit. "We'll keep trying. Carter said he was going to stop by after work today. Maybe he's got something new for us." Carter Smythe was a member of a local veteran's advocacy group. He stopped by every week bringing water and other supplies they needed and, as a representative of the advocacy group, assisted them where he could.

"Excuse me."

Six pairs of eyes shifted to an attractive, busty blonde wearing a low-cut white blouse and denim short shorts. She was standing next to several other young adults.

"Can we help you?" asked Tanker.

"Well, we'd like to offer you and all the veterans here some candy. It's just a small way we can show our appreciation for all you've done for our country."

"How nice of you! Just walk down the line of tents. Some vets are working but most are resting this time of day. They'll be happy to get some sweets."

The blonde looked over her shoulder at the others, nodding toward the tents. As they separated and made their way through the city, the blonde turned back to the six veterans sitting at the fire pit. Smiling, she offered them Starbursts, Jolly Rancher gummy bears, hard candies, bubble gum, and Tootsie Pops. They took their share, thanking her profusely, each grinning as she leaned over them, her ample bosom on full display.

The candy givers waved goodbye a few minutes later as they took their leave.

"Whew! That was a nice piece of–" began Carl.

"Careful there, Romeo," laughed Tanker and the others.

They drank water and munched on the candy, expressing appreciation for the kindness of those who passed by.

Tanker burped. "I don't feel very good." He rubbed his stomach. "Think I'm going to puke." He struggled to get up. "Whew, dizzy too. What the hell!"

"Can't take your candy?" Carl joked as he watched his friend grab onto a tree and vomit repeatedly. "Geez, Tanker, go get some rest. Be sure to drink some water, stay hydrated," he called out as Tanker stumbled the last few steps and disappeared inside his tent. "Poor guy." Carl shook his head, laughing with the others, as he popped more gummy bears into his mouth.

One by one, though, everyone began complaining of dizziness, nausea, drowsiness, or other symptoms, groaning as they made their way back to their tents.

Later that evening, Carter stopped by as promised. The first thing he noticed was how quiet it was. No one was in the common area. He couldn't hear any voices coming from the tents, no sounds at all. Usually, there was activity, movement, singing, something. He set the water and box of food down next to the fire pit and looked around.

Concerned, he stopped at the first tent and called out to Tanker. When there was no response, he peeked inside. Tanker was lying on his side on the ground in his own vomit. Carter rushed inside. Rolling Tanker onto his back, Carter glanced at his blue lips as he reached over and felt for a pulse on his neck. Nothing. He pulled out his phone and dialed 911 as he ran to the next tent, then the next. By the time the first responders arrived, Carter had checked half the tents. Three were alive, barely. He briefly conveyed what he had discovered then all hell broke loose. More ambulances arrived as well as the fire department, and the coroner wasn't far behind. Those who were still alive were taken to the hospital, and the dead were covered until their bodies could be removed.

The investigation as to what occurred began in earnest.

The news outlets caught wind of what was happening and were on the scene to report everything. Curious onlookers stood across the street, phones in hand recording anything that might be interesting.

The busty blonde and one of her companions were among the group of people, standing off to the side.

"Are you getting this?" she murmured.

He nodded, not looking away from his camera. "This video will be perfect."

"This is awesome!" She giggled, leaning over to kiss him on his ear. "I can't wait to hear who wins this challenge." She used her fingers to indicate quotes when she said *wins*. A menacing look crossed her face, turning it from one of beauty to one of evil. She sneered. "It serves them right if they all kick the bucket. When daddy left the Marines, he worked two jobs to support us. He didn't sit on his ass expecting handouts. The veterans I gave candy to all looked fit and able. They should go out and get a job."

"I've got what I need. Let me upload this to get the ball rolling then let's split." He pressed a few keys and within moments the video was posted on #RussianRouletteCandyChallenge.

CHAPTER SIXTEEN

Base of Operations, 8 miles west of Covington, PA
Thursday, January 13, 9:45 p.m.

KIRSTEN, SWORD, AND Felix had arrived fifteen minutes earlier, and the team was now sitting on the sofa and chairs in the living room, drinking beer and eating nachos. The large screen television was broadcasting a basketball game, but the sound was muted so they could talk. The candy orders Matey had placed were sitting on the coffee table, unopened, along with three plastic grocery-style bags.

"So how are we going to test the candy in those boxes?" asked Mali, as she leaned forward for a closer look at the box closest to her.

"And what's in the bags?" asked Matey.

Sword smiled. "I'm glad you asked. He opened up one of the bags and pulled out long, cylindrical tubes. "Everyone is familiar with epipens, right? They're for people who have severe allergies. These are similar to epipens but they contain Naloxone, otherwise known as Narcan."

"The drug used to reverse the effects of an opioid overdose," said Jake.

"That's right. Each cylinder contains two doses. I thought it might be a good idea for each of us to carry a cylinder with us at all times. It pays to be diligent."

"Great idea, right?" enthused Kirsten. "You should have seen where we went to get these."

Mali's eyebrows rose.

"Don't ask," said Sword. "A buddy of mine from the old days overdosed on heroin when I was visiting him in San Francisco last year. I found out he was addicted and went to see him to try to convince him to get help. He's a good man, just has severe PTSD, couldn't cope with what he witnessed and did in Afghanistan. He showed this to me, said he kept it with him at all times, just in case. Well, that 'just in case' happened the next day. I had gone to the store to pick up beer, was only gone maybe ten minutes. The liquor store was near his apartment. When I returned, he was overdosing, didn't even get the needle out of his arm. I scrambled to find the Narcan and injected him with it."

"My God," said Mali. "Did he survive?"

Face somber, he said, "Yes, luckily. He agreed to go into treatment when he was released from the hospital and he's back on his feet now. We stay in touch." He took a deep breath. "This is how you use these." He showed them how to pull the cap off the cylinder, remove one of the doses and punch it into the thigh. "There are enough for four doses each, that's two cylinders. Carry one with you at all times."

"Great job, Sword," said Jake. "Given what we're dealing with, having these with us is imperative. I'm glad you thought of it and took action." He tipped his beer bottle toward Sword in a salute.

Felix scratched his cheek while biting his lip. "Um, am I stating the obvious by saying that your friend wasn't able to inject himself. What makes you think we'll be able to if we begin to overdose?" He shuddered.

Jake responded. "Shooting up with heroin is fast-acting, the drug is injected directly into a vein. Feeling the effects of a drug while eating candy can take longer. Of course, we won't be eating candy, but there is a chance of encountering fentanyl in another form. We could touch it accidentally, for example. That being said, if you have to leave this house for any reason, take someone with you. We travel in pairs when feasible."

"Back to my initial question," began Mali.

"I can answer that," said Felix. He opened one of the two remaining bags on the coffee table, pulling out a small white box. "A couple of years ago, a company in Toronto developed test strips to detect traces of fentanyl. After its success, they expanded the capability of the strips to test other drugs like cocaine, and even some candies, for fentanyl. This box contains fifteen test strips, there are five boxes in this bag, for a total of seventy-five tests. They were surprisingly easy to locate and buy." He opened the other bag and pulled out surgical gloves, heavy-duty FFFP masks, and plastic face shields. "I also ordered this electric pill crusher and grinder from Amazon when I knew I was coming here." He pulled it out for everyone to inspect. "I was notified that it arrived when we were buying the Narcan pens, so we stopped by my place again on our way out of town to pick it up."

"Excellent. Tomorrow morning, let's inspect all bathrooms and determine which one has the best ventilation. That bathroom will become our testing location for the candy." He looked from Sword to Felix. "I want the two of you to manage this. Set up a table outside the bathroom door for the boxes of strips, masks, and gloves. I don't want anything to get contaminated. What goes inside the bathroom, stays there. We'll need some sort of sealable container for the used masks, gloves, tests strips, etcetera. Make sure both of you are in the bathroom when testing and a couple cylinders of the Narcan doses are there as well. Drive to Scranton and buy what you need to make it a safe, sealed environment. And since the grinder is going to turn the candy into powder, it has the potential of becoming airborne. Make sure you put it in a container of some sort. Keep the fan running and the window open when you're there."

Jake shifted his attention to Matey and Kirsten. "Find out when Los Rinches purchased Dandy Candy. Once we have the location of their facility, I want all the information you can find about it, number of employees, blueprints, shift change times, everything. Especially important are details of the structure itself and any architectural changes that may have taken place. Find out how they're distributing the orders. And continue dissecting the app. Matey, have you heard from Carson?"

Matey shook his head. "I've left a couple of messages.

He said it might take him some time. He'll get back to us when he has solid info."

Jake took a deep breath, letting it out slowly. "Mali and I are flying to Vegas tomorrow. Agent Whitby, with whom we worked on our last case involving Janet Simpson, is helping us. She called earlier to tell us that there are three facilities large enough to distribute candy, one in particular that she finds intriguing. We're going to check them out with her. We'll be gone two or three days. By the way, I contacted Slick and asked if he could divert one of the ghosts to make a visual pass of the three sites prior to our arrival tomorrow."

"Whoa," said Felix. "You contacted Jeff? And he actually agreed?"

"That's an interesting reaction. Why do you ask?"

"Well, he's been a bit of an ass since taking over the team, if you ask me. Riding high on his newfound power."

Jake frowned. "That doesn't sound like him."

"Are you talking about Jeff Cink?" asked Matey.

Jake nodded. "He joined our team a few months ago, was a real help too." Perplexed and looking at Felix, he asked, "Why do you say he's been an ass?"

Before Felix could answer, Sword asked, "What's a ghost?"

Kirsten explained how the *The Hunted Ones* app game allowed players to play the game anywhere in the world. The target and assassin could climb the Eiffel Tower in Paris or swim down the Grand Canyon in the game. The locations were real, not computer-generated.

Before his death, Hunter was trying to take the technology further by allowing a person to go anywhere in the world, through the game or some other means, and be there real-time without ever leaving their house. The target would be able to walk down a street past actual restaurants or stand next to real people. She puffed up with pride when she mentioned that she and Joe were able to create the ghost, and the team had used it successfully. The primary limitation was that the ghost couldn't go inside buildings. That part of the original code in *The Hunted Ones* game was left untouched.

"Holy shit!" exclaimed Sword.

"So he's willing to help?" asked Felix.

"Yes. He wasn't surprised that I was pursuing the case, given dad's murder, and said he'd help wherever he could. They're using all four ghosts in the new case they're working on but he's going to divert one early tomorrow morning. Slick will contact Agent Whitby for the addresses of the three facilities, and the ghost will recon them. He'll send a text with any information he can glean." Jake glanced at his watch. "It's late and we have an early flight. Sword, I want you and Felix to drive us to the Scranton airport."

Before Sword could answer, a flash of red on the television caught Mali's eye. She snapped her fingers and pointed to the screen. "Someone turn up the sound."

"Breaking news, and in case you're just joining us, twenty-nine homeless veterans died from an overdose at the Veterans Row tent city in West Los Angeles earlier this afternoon. It is believed that forty-one veterans were living there at the time. Ten others are being treated at the nearby VA medical center and are expected to live. Two veterans informed police that a group of young adults in their twenties were passing out candy to everyone. They had not eaten theirs, instead placing it in their tents for later as they were heading to their usual corner six blocks away to ask passersby for money. By the time they returned, the police were already there. The two were taken to the hospital and tested, as a precautionary measure. They were released a couple of hours later suffering no ill effects." The reporter put her finger up to her ear. "Just in, we have reports that a video of the scene was posted on #RussianRouletteCandyChallenge." She shook her head and paused, going completely still, her mouth falling open. Blinking a few times, she cleared her throat. "The implication that this was deliberately done for a game is just too hard to fathom." She wiped her brow. "We'll have more on this developing story later, as the facts come in. Gary?"

Kirsten wiped her eyes. "How could someone do that to unsuspecting veterans, to anyone?" she choked out.

Jake's lip curled. He stood and turned away. "We're leaving at six." He stormed down the hall and slammed the bedroom door shut.

CHAPTER SEVENTEEN

McCarran International Airport, Las Vegas
Friday, January 14, 12:25 p.m.

ANGELA WAVED TO them as they exited the airport. She was standing next to her car parked at the curb.

"It's good to see you again, Angela," said Mali, hugging her.

"You too. I'm glad you called." She shook Jake's hand. "Congratulations on your marriage, although I was sorry to hear about your dad." She motioned to the car and walked to the driver's side. "Have you eaten?"

Jake helped Mali into the rear seat of the sedan then sat in front next to Angela.

"We ate at the airport."

"Excellent, then we can head straight to the three facilities I mentioned." She pulled away from the curb. "We're going to the closest one first. The building is listed as a distribution center for toys. It's owned by a company called Lakeside Play, seems legit but the property has some pretty serious security and fencing. They want to keep people out. I haven't had a chance to research any of these other than preliminary information, but this is the one I was telling you about, Jake."

"We appreciate all you're doing, Angela." Mali opened her laptop, used the hot spot on her phone to connect to the internet, and began researching Lakeside Play.

They traveled southwest and twenty minutes later, Angela pulled to the side of the road across the street from the entrance, which was approximately fifteen feet across with a gate and guard shack. Looking inside the entrance, they spotted a large brick building with multiple smaller metal buildings on one side. The other side had docking stations for trucks. A truck was currently backed up to one of them, however it was too far away to determine what was being loaded or unloaded.

The facility was in an industrial park on the outskirts of town. Traffic was busy with mid-size trucks and eighteen wheelers pulling into and out of various businesses. Cars sped by, weaving around them, occasionally honking at the trucks. The facility encompassed an entire block that they circled, but an eight-foot metal privacy fence surrounded the entire property. Nothing was visible.

"From everything I'm reading about Lakeside Play, they're a legitimate company," said Mali, looking down at her screen. "They've been in business more than fifty years and provide toys to companies like Toys R Us and Walmart. They have twenty distribution centers across the states. This one is the biggest and they've owned it for more than ten years. Their headquarters are located closer to the Strip."

Angela said, "I don't know. Given the size and the

security, I think it's a good possibility, plus it's close to the airport and has easy access to travel routes for the trucks." She shrugged. "That's why I wanted to show it to you."

Jake took a deep breath and let it out slowly. "We'll need to get inside to make sure. Slick texted a video of a closeup of the main building, all four sides plus a wider view of the entire property. He seems to think this is a viable location as well, given the proximity to freeways. We'll consider next steps after seeing the other two locations." He glanced at Angela. "Let's go."

"The next location is northwest of here, about twenty miles past the Paiute Golf Resort. It's much more remote and secure. It'll take a little over an hour to get there."

Mali gripped the back of Jake's seat, her laptop forgotten, as Angela sped past cars, erratically moving from one lane to another, occasionally honking at the slower moving vehicles. "I thought traffic was bad in the City."

Angela's eyes shot to the rearview mirror. "Sorry about that, I'm used to getting where I want to go as quickly as possible." Grinning, she lifted her foot off the gas, slowing down to a few miles over the speed limit.

The conversation died down as the miles flew by, Angela occasionally pointing out things of interest.

"We exit ninety-five in two miles and, according to GPS, the second location is only twelve miles away, tucked in the hills from what I can tell. I've known of its existence, but I've never been there. The property is owned by a company called Systap, a tech company that builds storage systems for companies, databases or something. This location is supposedly a processing plant."

Mali had been staring out the window, enjoying the passing scenery. She pulled her laptop from the seat next to her, and quickly pressed some keys before saying, "I can't find any information on how long they've owned this property, but the company itself is solid."

Angela turned left after exiting the freeway and began climbing. The winding road was more of a narrow country lane. Even though no one else was on the road, the condition of it forced them to travel slowly. It was another twenty minutes before Angela indicated that their turn to the company was coming up on the right.

Rounding a corner, they arrived at the turn they were supposed to make but it was blocked off with a metal gate and a guard shack in front of and to the side of the gate. One guard was inside. Although not a privacy fence, the property was fenced similar to the previous location, from what they could tell. A large No Trespassing sign was posted on one side.

"Wow, I guess they don't want anyone inside. You can't see any buildings from here," said Angela.

"Hmmm." Mali rolled down her window and leaned her head out, trying to see beyond the fencing. "Technical espionage is a huge problem. It doesn't surprise me that they might not want any visitors." She rolled her window up and looked at Jake. "Anything useful from Jeff?"

"He sent a video from the ghost. It looks like there are three large buildings. Security is tight. Additional fencing surrounds the inner area and guards are posted at the entrance there, as well. He feels the location might be too remote considering how quickly the candy is distributed."

"Good point, although that much security seems extreme to me," said Mali, "even for a tech company."

"I was thinking the same thing," said Jake. "Head back to town, Angela. I want to check into the hotel, grab a bite to eat, then assess what we've learned. We can look at the third location in the morning, if needed."

As soon as he saw them, the guard had stepped outside of the shack. When they didn't leave right away, he started walking toward them.

Angela rolled down her window and waved. "I'm sorry, we took a wrong turn and we're lost."

He flipped up the safety strap on his gun's holster, continuing to advance. Pointing behind them, he said, "Leave."

Alarmed, Mali said, "Whoa, this guy means business."

"Thank you." Angela waved to him again then put the car in reverse and they left. She grinned at Jake as she drove away. "I guess they don't like unannounced visitors."

By the time they returned to Vegas, it was almost five. Angela dropped them off at the Treasure Island Hotel & Casino on the Strip, saying that the FBI got special rates there. She thought they'd enjoy exploring the Strip when they needed a break. Waving goodbye, she said she'd pick them up the next morning at nine.

Mali and Jake walked into the dim interior of the hotel, briefly stopping to allow their eyes to adjust. The cacophony of noise assailed Mali, from the slot machines to the cheers of a group playing craps, as they wound around tables, chairs, gaming tables, and the throng of people, to get to the reservation desk. Once in their room, they unpacked, took quick showers and changed, then rode the elevator back to the lobby to find a place to dine. By mutual agreement, they didn't discuss anything about the case during dinner. They didn't dawdle, however, as both wanted to get to work.

They were approaching their room, arm in arm, when Jake suddenly stopped, tensing. Surprised, Mali glanced at him. He put a finger to his mouth then pointed at their door. It was open, just a crack. Pushing Mali behind him, they crept toward the door. Hearing some rustling, Jake motioned for Mali to stay then reached for the gun usually tucked in the back of his pants. It wasn't there.

Frowning and hands fisted, he shook his head once then, in one fluid movement, he ducked low and slammed through the door. Mali peeked inside but it was too dark to see anything other than shadows. She heard grunts and fists connecting with body parts. She jumped when she heard glass shattering. She assumed the lamp on the nightstand crashed to the ground. It was the only accessory made of glass in the room. All of a sudden, a man dressed in jeans and a navy blue hoodie, shot out of the room barreling into Mali. His hands automatically reached out to grasp her shoulders to keep from falling. She gasped and, in that brief moment, saw his face. His cold brown eyes narrowed before he shoved her to the side and sprinted down the hall. Jake wasn't far behind him.

"You okay?"

"Yes, go!"

As Jake raced after him, Mali took a few calming breaths before walking into the room and switching on the light. It had been turned upside down. Their clothes were haphazardly tossed everywhere, and her makeup and other toiletries in the bathroom were scattered across the counter and floor. The bed had been stripped and the mattress was half-on and half-off the bed frame. The broken lamp was lying on the tiled floor next to the mattress.

Mali was sitting in a chair by the window when Jake returned. He took in the scene then walked over to Mali, squatting in front of her.

She was pale but composed. "You're bleeding," she said, using the bottom of her blouse to wipe the blood from the corner of his mouth.

Jake placed his hand on hers, stopping her movement. "The son-of-a-bitch got away. I'd say we're making some people nervous."

"How can–"

Jake gave a cautionary shake of his head then assessed the damage. "Check to see if anything has been taken, then pack up. We're leaving." He stood up.

When she continued to sit there, he reached down and pulled her to her feet. "Go."

Jake put the mattress back on the bed frame and checked the suitcase for bugs then placed it on the bed.

Mali began picking up the clothes. As she placed them on the bed, Jake inspected them for bugs as well. When each item was cleared, she packed them in the suitcase She grimaced as she picked up her underwear, pausing to look down at the black lace in her hand. *I doubt I can wear this ever again. Washing may not be enough.* She sighed then stepped into the bathroom to pack the toiletries. Jake called Agent Whitby as Mali opened the safe to remove and pack her laptop and some pieces of jewelry.

They walked out of the hotel fifteen minutes later. Agent Whitby was waiting at the entrance.

"My God, are you guys okay? What the hell happened?"

"We're both fine," said Jake, after helping Mali into the car then seating himself in front. He turned sideways to look at Angela as she pulled away from the curb. "Someone knows we're here."

"How is that possible?" asked Mali. "We only arrived this morning."

"You flew commercial, right?"

Jake nodded. "Damn it." He rubbed his face.

"And we used our real names." Mali groaned as she looked out the window. "But who has the resources to track us from all over the U.S.?"

"You mean besides the cartel that makes millions of dollars every day?" growled Angela. "The corruption extends well into our borders. People can be paid off here as well as in Mexico." She pounded the steering wheel with her hand. "Did they find anything?"

"There wasn't anything to find," said Mali. "I had only just begun researching the locations and we haven't spoken to any team members for an update. My computer was in the safe, however, and we had our cell phones with us."

"They may have been trying to scare us away." Jake took a deep breath and let it out slowly. "Take us to a small hotel off the Strip. I need to make some calls and I want to be in an inconspicuous place."

Angela nodded and pulled into a small motel four miles away. Thanking her, they requested a later pickup in the morning. They planned to take care of some business first. Angela agreed to pick them up at ten o'clock.

They checked in, paying cash, then walked up the stairs and into the room.

"Jake," Mali set her toiletries case down on the bathroom counter then stared at him through the mirror. He walked up behind her and placed his hands on her shoulders. "If someone really did track us from the flight, then they know we're staying somewhere in the Scranton area. The team may not be safe."

"That's possible." He murmured, staring at her. "What if that isn't the case?"

"What do you mean? Do you think someone on our team—?"

"No. I trust them completely, which is why I'll call Matey in a few minutes and tell them to pack up now and leave immediately, out of an abundance of caution." He paused, staring into her eyes. "The only other people who knew we were coming here are Jeff and Angela."

CHAPTER EIGHTEEN

McCarran International Airport, Las Vegas
Saturday, January 15, 12:45 p.m.

"ARE YOU SURE I can't do anything more for you?" asked Angela as they arrived at the airport. They spent a couple of hours driving to, and assessing, the third location. After seeing it, they all felt that it wasn't a large enough facility nor did the security appear to be sufficient. The video from the ghost that Jeff had sent seemed to confirm their assessment.

Mali smiled and shook her head. "You've already done so much for us, Angela. You've shown us three possible locations for the distribution center, although we've narrowed it down to two, schlepping us all over the place. We can't thank you enough." She reached forward, placing her hand on Angela's shoulder and squeezed.

"This quick visit has been very productive and eye-opening. We have a good start for moving forward, thanks to you." Jake smiled at her. "We couldn't have achieved so much in such a short time without your help."

"Are you kidding? I'd do anything to help you guys." Angela pulled to the curb and turned off the engine. She turned sideways, resting her left arm on the steering wheel. "When will you be back, and is there anything I can do while you're gone?" She glanced from Jake to Mali.

"We'll regroup with the team and review all of this information then formulate a plan of action. I'm not sure when we'll return but we'll contact you as soon as we have a date." Jake reached for the car door handle. "Slick said he'd have a ghost recon the two sites every couple of days, whenever he can pull it away from their case without notice. There's nothing for you to do at this point."

Angela nodded. "Okay. Be careful. It's risky flying commercial again. Stay alert."

"Will do. Thanks again, Angela." Jake shook her hand. "We'll be in touch." He opened the door and stepped out of the car, moving to the passenger door and opening it for Mali.

Mali waved as Angela pulled away, then they turned and walked into the terminal, making their way to the check-in counter.

"I just can't believe Angela's involved."

Jake remained silent as they shuffled through the line. After checking in, they waited in another line to go through TSA security. Twenty minutes later, they were at the gate for their flight. All seats in the waiting area were taken, except for a few singles. Mali and Jake walked to the next gate and sat down.

Jake covertly observed the people who were walking to and fro. Some were rushing through the terminal saying 'Excuse me' over their shoulders as they nudged people out of their way. Others meandered through, obviously with time on their hands before their flight.

"I want to wait thirty minutes to ensure no one has followed us inside," said Jake.

"Do you think Angela suspected anything?"

"No, but I want to make sure before we pick up the van Matey rented for us."

"I hate deceiving her."

Jake glanced down at her then pulled her close. "So do I. But we can't afford to trust anyone at this point. Better to let them think we're none the wiser, which is why I asked Jeff to continue to surveil the two locations with the ghost when he can. If we're wrong about them, they'll never know."

"Better to be safe than sorry, I suppose."

He leaned back and half-closed his eyes, giving the appearance of resting while he continued to people watch. "What time do the others arrive?"

"The jet arrives at two-forty. We can make our way to the executive entrance for private jets after we pick up the van. Had I known father had put so much money into my account, we would have flown privately before." She leaned back, laying her head on Jake's shoulder and closing her eyes.

At two o'clock, they walked down to baggage claim and out the door, crossing the street to pick up the van.

Sword, Matey, Kirsten, and Felix were walking out

the door, with all of their baggage in tow, as Jake pulled up to the curb. Felix's arm was in a sling and he had bruises on his face. Kirsten was limping.

"What happened? Are you okay?" Mali was out of the van in an instant, hugging her friend.

"We'll tell you when we're on the move," growled Matey, flinging open the side door and climbing into the back.

Jake opened the back doors and helped Sword place the equipment inside as everyone else crammed into the van. "The load looks light," he noted. Sword's lips thinned but he said nothing, just turned and got into the front passenger seat.

As soon as the door was closed, Kirsten blurted, "We were attacked as we were getting ready to leave."

"What!" Mali's jaw dropped in shock.

Jake's eyes shot to Sword, then to Matey, through the rear-view mirror.

Matey explained. "We were almost finished packing everything when all hell broke loose. Two men entered from the front, guns blazing, and three others from the rear. Kirsten was in her bedroom packing her clothes, Sword was in the john, and Felix and I were in the living room and kitchen."

Kirsten shuddered. "As soon as I heard shots, I dropped what I was doing and snuck to the window to see if anyone was outside. Not seeing anyone, I climbed out the window. I knew Sword had already stored his bag of weapons in the trunk. I tripped and fell, twisting my ankle, when I ran to the car." She rolled her eyes.

"It was still in the barn where we always kept it." She grimaced. "I'm still shaking. I grabbed a few guns and returned as fast as I could, but Sword and Matey had already killed the five men."

Matey continued with the encounter. "Felix and I took cover in the kitchen behind the island. I grabbed some knives and was able to slow two down, and--"

Felix interrupted him. "By slowing them down, he means he nailed them in their throats."

Mali glanced at Felix, who was sitting next to her, and smiled, despite the circumstances. Matey was obviously his hero.

"Sword surprised the other three. It was over in a few minutes. We didn't realize that Felix's shoulder was grazed by a bullet until after we had ensured that there were no other attackers." Matey finished without missing a beat, ignoring the comment Felix made.

"Do you know who they were or how they found you?" asked Jake, as he headed out of town.

Sword answered. "They must have followed us from Scranton, your flight to Vegas was probably flagged. They obviously took time to recon our ops base then bring in help. They all looked like Mexicans."

"They looked like mean SOBs," stated Kirsten. "Shaved heads, scarred faces, tattoos everywhere. They looked evil."

"Thank God you're all okay," said Mali.

"Thank *you* for making arrangements for that private jet," said Matey. "We wouldn't have been able to bring our gear on a commercial flight. As it is, two of my monitors were shot and we had to leave a few weapons plus the 3D printer behind."

"They shot my printer to hell," groused Sword.

Matey glanced at Sword before continuing. "We weren't sure if anyone else was coming so we grabbed what we could and split."

"Where are we going?" asked Felix.

"We booked a ranch northwest of the Strip, about thirty minutes past Nellis Air Force Base. It should fit our needs and we'll be an hour from the location we believe is where the distribution center is set up," said Jake.

"You've already ruled out the other two locations?" asked Kirsten.

Mali grinned as she turned to look at Kirsten who was sitting beside her. "The second location we went to, a tech company called Systap, is remote, well-guarded, and with multiple buildings that could accommodate their operation. But the kicker is that *systap* is *patsys* spelled backward."

"I don't get it," said Kirsten, a blank look on her face.

"Agent Whitby told me that lollipops are sometimes called patsy's in certain parts of the country."

"You're kidding."

Mali laughed. "That's what I said."

"Cool," said Felix.

"We should arrive in about ten minutes. As soon as we get there, let's drop our things off then grab a bite to eat. We can set everything up when we get back. Sword, Mali and I ditched our phones at the airport. We'll need new burners." Jake pulled off the interstate as he spoke. Fifteen minutes later, they turned down a narrow dirt lane and drove approximately one mile before a sprawling ranch house appeared in a small valley filled with straw-colored buffalo grass. Agave plants lined the front entrance along the porch, their spiny-edged blue-gray leaves stretching in all directions.

"I love the desert," said Kirsten, looking around. She grabbed a bag from the back and headed inside.

As Jake followed everyone in, he said, "There are six rooms, take your pick. Let's meet at the van in ten."

* * *

The drive to Moapa Valley, a small town further east, took less than twenty minutes. They agreed on pizza and stopped at a place called Pirates Landing.

"It smells divine in here," exclaimed Mali when she stepped inside. She inhaled deeply. "I'm starving."

A waitress called out to them from a few tables over. "Take a seat anywhere folks."

"Let's grab the large booth in the corner." Jake pointed to a booth on the other end of the restaurant. "We'll have a little privacy and can talk," he said, leading the way. They passed one booth with a family of five, just as the mother attempted to pacify her fussy toddler, and walked by mostly-empty tables, before sliding into the booth at the far end of the room. No one sat near them, and they could observe all who entered.

After ordering drinks and their pizzas, the conversation turned to updates.

"I spoke with Carson last night," began Matey.

Jake's eyebrows rose.

"He was told by his informant that Armano's whereabouts are unknown as he doesn't stay in the same place more than two nights, and they are working with the Chinese in two ways. The Chinese are sending counterfeit pills, like oxycodone spiked with fentanyl, to the cartel in Mexico. The cartel, in turn, moves the pills up through the border. But they're losing money and getting frustrated as the border patrol confiscates more and more shipments. The Chinese also send the ingredients for fentanyl to the cartel, and they make it for their candy operation. Carson isn't sure where the ingredients are taken once they arrive in Mexico, but he was told that Armano feels that candy is the future, especially given the problems they're having at the border."

Mali frowned. "So is he making the spiked candy in Mexico and shipping it north, or is he shipping the ingredients north then making the fentanyl and lacing it with the candy here?"

"Carson didn't know."

Kirsten asked, "How are the spiked pills being discovered at the border? Can dogs smell fentanyl like they do other drugs? And if that's the case, wouldn't spiked candy also be discoverable?"

"Good questions. I can check on that when we get back to the ranch," said Mali, making a note.

Jake tapped his fingers on the table. "We'll get more answers once we recon the Systap property, at least I'm hoping we do. The ghost showed three buildings on the property. Are all of them being used and, if so, for what purpose?"

"I have a hard time believing that they're actually making the fentanyl. I mean, here in our country? They must ship it in and store it in one of the buildings." Felix frowned before gulping down his beer.

Matey rubbed his chin. "Storing it would apply whether they ship in spiked candy, or if they ship in clean candy and spike it on site."

Jake motioned with his hand to stop talking when he noticed the waitress heading over with their pizzas.

"Here you go," she said, smiling. She set them down in the middle of the table. "More drinks?" When everyone nodded, she excused herself, returning a few moments later with refreshed sodas and beer.

Conversation stopped as everyone attacked the food with gusto.

Jake wiped his mouth and took a slug of beer. He leaned forward, everyone else did the same. "Okay. Let's get everything set up when we return to the ranch. Sword, Matey, first thing tomorrow, I want the two of you to purchase any additional gear we'll need to recon Systap, including night-vision goggles, binoculars, bugs for us to plant, assuming we get inside any of the buildings, you know the drill. I also want good communications. We'll need to be able to stay in touch with the team at the ranch."

Sword frowned. "Um, where exactly are we supposed to get this stuff? Back in Vegas?"

Jake shook his head. "Look east or north. I don't want to take any chances going back."

"Got it." Felix smiled, looking up from the laptop he had brought with him. At everyone's questioning look, he said, "I just searched for places east of the ranch that might have stores carrying the stuff Sword and Matey will need. Mesquite has a Home Depot and a gun shop. But St. George has multiple gun and ammo shops. It's about two hours west and north of the ranch, in Utah, probably your best bet." He looked at Jake. "If it's all right with you, I'd like to go with them. There's some technology I'd like to have on hand in case we need it."

Jake shook his head, signaling the waitress for the bill. "Give your list to Matey. I need you to track down plans for all buildings on the Systap property then I have a special task for you and Kirsten tomorrow."

"I need some monitors and other technical gear as well," added Matey.

Jake glanced at Matey when they got to the van. "I noticed a car rental place as we were driving here. I'm going to drop you and Kirsten off. There will be times when we need a second vehicle. Rent a sedan. Hoop is our bank."

Mali reached into her bag, pulling out multiple fifties and hundreds, and handed them to Matey.

Felix whistled. "As long as you're passing it around." He wiggled his eyebrows up and down.

Mali laughed. Sword reached over and punched him.

"Ow!" Felix rubbed his arm. "That was my one good arm, I'll have you know."

Sword rolled his eyes as Jake drove a block past the car rental then pulled to the curb.

As soon as Matey and Kirsten stepped out of the van, Jake pulled away without looking back.

The team spent the rest of the evening setting up the ranch for their operation. Since they were all eager to get the show on the road, they turned in shortly after eleven.

Jake was brushing his teeth in the bathroom when Mali walked in to wash her face.

"Do you think they're making the fentanyl in one of the buildings?"

Jake spit out the toothpaste. "That's what I'd do. The ingredients would be easy to hide and would not be detectable by the drug dogs at the border. It's the perfect set up. We'll know soon enough."

CHAPTER NINETEEN

Nevada ranch
Sunday, January 16, 9:00 p.m.

JAKE CALLED THE team to the kitchen island for final preparations.

"Felix, Kirsten, any problems this afternoon tagging Agent Whitby's car?"

Kirsten shook her head. "She went to lunch at a swanky place off the Strip, met a man there. I went inside and pretended that I was waiting for a friend. I couldn't see the man, unfortunately, his back was to me. While I was inside, Felix placed a tracker on her SUV."

"No one saw you?" Jake asked Felix.

He shook his head. "There were a few people heading to and from the restaurant, but no one was near her vehicle. I dropped the keys as I walked by the back of the car, just in case anyone was watching me. The tracker is on a magnetic strip so it was easy to slap it on the inside of the left rear bumper, grab my keys, and keep going."

"We pulled out of the lot and parked across the street to wait for her to leave," continued Kirsten. "We wanted to test it the standard way. She walked out of the restaurant alone about forty-five minutes later and drove away."

Felix gave a thumbs up signal. "It worked like a charm. We were able to track her back to her house, staying a comfortable half-mile back." Felix paused as he punched a few keys on his laptop that was on the counter in front of him. "However, here's the really cool part." He held the tablet out to show them.

"What are we looking at?" asked Mali.

"The flashing icon is the pinpoint location of her car, which is currently at her house. Now, if you click the icon, we can zoom in for a visual." He clicked the icon as he spoke. Agent Whitby's car was in her driveway and a young woman walking her dog passed by as they watched.

"Whoa! How the hell did you do that?" asked Jake.

Grinning from ear to ear, Felix said, "Remember that satellite Hunter used for his game that we confiscated along with all of his other technology?"

"You mean the satellite we use for the ghosts that Jeff currently has deployed for their case?" asked Mali.

Kirsten beamed. "We accessed it through the backdoor. We're piggy-backing off it."

"Brilliant," said Matey.

"Wait a minute," said Jake. "Won't they know we're using it?"

"Only if they're looking," said Felix. "And the only person who might look is Joe."

Mali frowned. "Do we need to be concerned?"

"We can trust Joe," said Kirsten. "Like Felix and me, he's pretty upset with what's happened. And he's savvy enough, with Felix and I gone, to realize who's using it." She stared at Jake. "We can trust him not to tell anyone, at least before he tries to contact us."

Jake looked up toward the ceiling, lips pursed. Dropping his eyes to Kirsten, he said, "I don't want to wait for him to discover it and possibly let the cat out of the bag. Call him tonight. Less is more in terms of what you tell him."

Kirsten nodded. "I'm sure he'll help any way he can."

Jake nodded. "Sword, Matey, are we ready to go?"

"The van's loaded with our gear and we've picked the spot where we'll hide the van. It's about ten clicks to the property," said Sword. "Matey downloaded the plans Felix found, as well as the additional info Hoop was able to provide, onto his mini-iPad and two others."

Matey handed a mini-iPad to Sword and to Jake and showed them where the information was located.

Jake nodded. "This looks good. Let's bring up the plans one more time." They spent the next thirty minutes reviewing the plans and determining the best place for each to position themselves.

"It looks pretty standard," said Matey. "All buildings seem to be warehouses, open space except for some rooms, perhaps offices, on the sides. We won't know if they've modified the insides of each unless and until we can get inside."

When the three were all in agreement and comfortable with their plan, Jake turned to Mali. "Do you have any new information?"

Mali nodded. "Felix hacked into the border patrol

database and sent me their entry logs, both video and agent entries, for the last nine months. I haven't been able to look at everything in detail yet, but I've noticed a pattern of a particular logged entry. Every two weeks, like clockwork, two eighteen wheelers enter the U.S. through the El Paso border. The company listed is S-LR with contents of confection supplies. The same border agent signs off on it." She looked up from what she had been reading on her laptop. "I think S-LR stands for Systap Los Rinches and the contents are the candy, fentanyl, or both. Just before this meeting, Felix and I were able to find the trucks on video that correlate with the online entries. We sent a picture of one to you. According to the logs, two trucks passed through the border yesterday afternoon."

Jake nodded. "With luck, we'll be in place to observe if any arrive. Thanks Hoop." He paused. "Sword, Matey and I will be gone for at least two days, possibly more. Felix and Kirsten, keep tabs on Agent Whitby and tell me when she's on the move and where she goes. Hoop, continue to research Systap. Also, try to figure out how they're delivering product to the customer." He stared at each team member. "Let's do this."

* * *

Ten kilometers from Systap
Monday, January 17, 12:10 a.m.

Sword drove past the exit on ninety-five that would lead to Systap, instead taking the third exit past it. "According to the map, there should be a dirt road on the other side of ninety-five that will take us to the base of the hill, below and to the north of Systap." He turned left and drove under the freeway.

"Where does this road lead?" asked Jake.

Looking at the map on his iPad, Matey said, "Looks like it dead-ends. Could have been a fire break at one time."

One hundred yards after they drove under the freeway, the concrete road turned to packed dirt. Sword crept along to minimize the noise the van made and to avoid the potholes. Even so, the road had ridges and they bounced around as if there was a constant stream of bump strips, like those used when traffic controllers want to slow you down because of construction. It was pitch black, the moonless night and trees alongside the road hiding them from view. The only lights were the headlights of the van, which were kept on low beam so as not to carry.

They drove in silence for twenty minutes, when they rounded a corner and the road ended abruptly at the base of the hill. Sword cursed, even though he was going slow and there was no need to slam on the brakes.

"According to the map, Systap is two hills over, just shy of ten clicks."

All three looked from left to right, deciding where to hide the van.

"Pull off the road about twenty yards on the right side." Jake gestured with his hand. "It looks like a good place. I want to change and be out of here in fifteen."

Sword moved the van as instructed and all three exited the vehicle. Opening the back, they pulled three military-grade desert-colored backpacks out and set them on the ground. Stripping out of their jeans and shirts, they quickly dressed in desert camo gear.

"Feels like the old days," said Sword, grinning.

Their civilian clothing was tossed inside, and the van doors were shut. Each reached into their backpack and pulled out a small canister. Opening it, they applied the ceremonial desert brown paint on their faces.

"Let's check our communications." Jake inserted the Bluetooth earpiece into his ear, Sword and Matey following suit. They confirmed that they could hear each other and Felix as well. Mali, Kirsten, and Felix agreed to take four-hour shifts to give each other a chance to sleep. Felix had first watch.

They covered the van with camouflage netting, put on their night vision goggles, then took off. The climb over the first hill was slow-going. The terrain was thick with brush, trees, and some small cacti that they had to navigate around. The biggest problem, however, were the small rocks covering the ground. Every step they took seemed to echo loudly. They were forced to step slowly and with intention to minimize the noise they made. It was like a low crawl but on two feet. They reached the other side of the hill, roughly seven kilometers in ninety minutes. At the base of the hill leading up to Systap, they stopped.

"Shit, that was brutal," whispered Sword. "We'll be lucky to be in position by daybreak."

Jake took a sip of water from his canteen, frown-ing. "Let's not waste any time. Matey, as we discussed, go east to the base of the hill then up toward their front entrance. Sword, head west and up toward their rear. That should put you closest to the small building. I'll continue south straight up. When you reach the border of the property, continue toward the inner fence, if it's safe to do so, and find a place to hunker down. That's our preferred first recon position. We'll decide how to proceed within the property once we've scoped things out. Plan to be there all day. We'll get some rest once we are in position and check in. Be careful."

Sword and Matey gave a thumbs up and took off. Jake watched them leave then looked up the hill. Taking a deep breath, he began his ascent.

By three-thirty, Jake was standing in a copse of trees five feet from the outer fence. On this end of the prop-erty, the fence wasn't as formidable as at the entrance. Vertical steel beams stood six feet high, approximately ten feet apart. Barbed wire ran horizontally between the beams, six inches between each horizontal strand from the ground up to the top of the beams. The second fence pro-tecting the buildings inside was just twenty yards from his position. All three buildings were visible in the distance.

Jake ensured there were no security guards patrol-ling, then tossed some rocks at the fence. They bounced off, landing in the dirt below. The fence was not electric. Staying within the trees and brush, Jake walked parallel to the outer fence until he spotted a berm close to the inner fence, a good place to hunker down. Searching along the outer fence line, he noticed a few trees clustered together just inside the fence. He crept to a steel beam that was positioned behind the trees, knelt down, and snipped the two lowest horizontal barbed wires from the fence using wire cutters he pulled from his backpack. They dropped to the ground without a sound. Jake's hope was that if guards patrolled the area, the trees would hide this part of the fence and the cuts would go unnoticed.

Placing the wire cutters back into his pack, he shoved it under the fence then scooted under it himself. Lying down on his stomach, he inched toward the backside of the berm. Once behind it, he removed the small shovel from his backpack. Fortunately, the terrain inside the property was more dirt, less rocks. He dug a hole two-foot deep and eight feet long so he'd be tucked in along the back side of the berm allowing him to lie down. He only had to lift his head a few inches to look inside the inner sanctum. Crawling back to the outer gate with a small branch, he backed his way to the berm swinging the branch on the dirt from left to right to cover his tracks. Once back in the hole, he covered himself with the dirt he dug and nearby brush.

In position, he turned on his comm. "Pirate in position. Report."

"Matey here. I crossed the first fence line, and I'm twelve yards from the inner fence. The road leading in is to my right, approximately thirty yards. I have a clear view of anything that enters or exits, and building one is in my sights."

"I just arrived at the rear of the property," said Sword. "The climb was almost vertical. Security is light as a result. The interior of the operation reaches to this fence line, there is no other fence. There's a ledge forty feet to my left that's below the base of the fence. I should have a good view of building three which is twenty yards away. I'll settle there."

"Good. I'm lying behind a berm ten yards from the inner fence. From my position, I can watch all three buildings. Building two is closest. There are no guards patrolling between the two fence lines, but multiple guards are positioned outside each building and a few more are walking the perimeter of the inner fence. It's almost four. Get some rest. Check in at eight."

At seven-thirty, Matey's voice came across the comm line. "Two eighteen wheelers are rolling in. They appear to be the same as the picture Hoop gave us. I'm live streaming it to the ranch."

Mali said, "Good morning. I see them and, yes, they're the same. Send us pictures of whatever you can."

"The first truck is continuing past building one, but the second truck is pulling to a stop beside it."

Jake said, "Noted. It looks like the first truck is going to building three. What do you see, Sword?"

"The warehouse door of building three has opened and two people are waiting for the truck to back up. I can zoom in pretty close with these binoculars. I've got some good pics of the two goons, and they're wearing hazmat gear. I'll snap additional pictures as they unload. They're coming to you, Hoop."

"Good. We're ready on our end."

"The truck is still unloading at building one, but I'm sending some pictures now. It's hard to tell what's in the crates. There's writing on the sides. I couldn't read it, but you may be able to zoom in once you download the pictures."

"Thanks Matey."

Sword whispered, "They're beginning to unload the second truck now, a few crates, no visible markings. Wait, one of the goons looks pissed. He's gesturing with his arms and looks to be shouting at the driver. He just yanked on rubber gloves and is prying open one of the crates right on the loading dock. Hang on a sec. I'm switching to live stream." Sword whistled softly. "Do you see that?"

Mali's voice was barely above a whisper. "He's holding up a bag with a hole in it. It looks like granules are coming out of the bag. Great zoom capability by the way." Her voice rose in pitch, and she was speaking faster. "Is everyone looking at this? The bag says 'citric acid'."

"Damn," said Jake. "They're making the fentanyl here."

CHAPTER TWENTY

By four o'clock, the team had confirmed multiple aspects of the cartel's operation.

During the day, two other eighteen-wheelers arrived, all unloading crates into building one. They were then loaded with boxes and left. While Jake realized that they wouldn't be able to get inside any of the buildings— security was too tight—they were able to determine that the crates unloaded at building one were full of candy and the building was a warehouse where the candy was stored. They made an assumption that it also housed the business side of the operation where online orders were fulfilled by staff who then boxed them up for shipment. The team believed the boxes loaded onto the eighteen wheelers were those online orders. They weren't sure where the trucks went and how those orders were delivered but knowing that was a lower priority.

Their belief that the fentanyl was made in building three was confirmed as the day progressed. Everyone who entered the building wore hazmat gear and placed N95 masks over their mouths and noses as they walked in, with plastic shields over their whole face.

While they couldn't confirm what occurred in building two, it was a logical assumption that the candy was spiked for the illegal orders there. Crates of candy from building one were moved there with a fork lift throughout the day. In addition, sealed plastic containers were rolled from building three to building two on a trolley, which they believe held the fentanyl.

Earlier in the day, a smaller truck arrived on property and off-loaded barrels at building two. The team was unable to verify the contents of the barrels, but the first two rows of them were moved to the side and the barrels behind them were taken into the building. The barrels that were set aside were then placed back inside the truck, and the truck left. The assumption was that those barrels had legitimate product inside, in case they were searched, and the ones behind them contained the other drugs that could be ordered from the app: cocaine, meth, MDMA, and heroin. Closed brown order boxes were moved to building one, they believed, for shipment.

"I think it would be wise to spend one more night here. When it gets dark, we'll relocate. Perhaps we can glean something new from different viewpoints."

Sword groaned. "Pirate, we have solid intel. One more night isn't going to make much difference. Besides, I'm sick of beef jerky, fruit, and nuts. I'd like a juicy steak."

Jake chuckled. "You'll get your steak soon enough, Sword. I just think–"

"Sorry to interrupt," began Matey. "But we've got

company coming in. Two black SUVs with dark, tinted windows."

Jake looked through his binoculars. "Got 'em. They're pulling up to building one. My view is blocked, Matey. Your view should be unobstructed. Live stream it so we can all see."

A moment later, Jake, Sword, and the team at the ranch were all watching as one person exited the first car and went straight into the building. Two other men stepped out of the second car and spoke with a man who had walked up to them.

Mali gasped. "That's Armano!"

"Shit, zoom in Matey," said Jake.

Mali gasped again. "The second guy looks like– Jake, that's Matt Spencer, Cenzo to the cartel. He's the guy who spotted you in Cabo."

Jake fumed. "Dammit! The leader and one of his trusted henchmen, right under our nose. Who was the third guy in the hoodie?"

"No clue. He went straight into the building," said Matey.

"We have to take advantage of this gift," stated Jake.

"Pirate, I know you want to get this guy, we all do. But there are only three of us here. And there's a shitload of fire power over there."

"I know, Matey. We can't take him out here. But we also can't let this opportunity slip by. He only stays in one place one or two nights. Who knows where he's headed next?"

"Can't you just tail him when he leaves?" asked Mali.

"No, as remote as this area is, they'll spot us immediately." He paused. "But we can wait on the road leading to Systap, close to ninety-five, and take him there."

"It could work," said Sword. "But we'd have to book it back to the van, and what if he leaves before we get there? How will we even know if he's left?"

"Sword, get your stuff together and head back to the van now. I won't be far behind you. Matey, stay here and keep us informed of any movement. Felix, get in the car and head to Paiute Golf Resort. It's off ninety-five, fifteen miles before the road leading to Systap. As soon as it's dark, head to ninety-five, Matey. Contact Felix and he'll pick you up. Mali and Kirsten, continue keeping tabs on Angela's whereabouts and also on us. Keep the comm lines open. Everyone clear?" After receiving affirmatives from everyone, Jake carefully extracted himself from the property and made his way down the hill. When he felt he was far enough away, he picked up his pace, slowing down only when he walked on rocks.

It took half the time to get back to the van. Sword was already there. He had changed clothes and wiped off most of the paint. Jake threw his pack in the back, changed, and then wiped off the paint as Sword drove back to the main road. They had just entered the freeway when Matey spoke up.

"One of the SUVs just left the property. I couldn't tell who got in, but the SUV will be down the hill in fifteen."

"Good. We'll be in place in five. Get out of there as soon as it's safe to do so. Felix, where are you?"

"I pulled into Paiute about twenty minutes ago. I'll wait here until Matey calls."

"Where is Angela, Hoop?"

"She's been at work all day. I assume she'll be headed home soon."

"Good. Everyone stay alert."

Sword exited the freeway and turned onto the winding country lane.

"I remember a couple of entrances to private properties a mile or two up the road. Pull into one of them. As soon as the SUV gets close, pull out. We'll take whoever is inside alive, if possible. Hopefully, it's Armano and we can end this." Jake rolled down his window then reached behind him and pulled out his Sig Sauer. Sword's semi-automatic was on the floor at his feet.

A half mile up the road, Sword found a small dirt road leading to a gate. He pulled in and turned the van around, with the front facing out. He backed as close to the gate as possible so the SUV wouldn't see them until it was too late.

"I hear a car coming, and it's moving fast," said Sword.

Jake saw a flash of black thirty yards up the road. "Go!"

Sword hit the gas and the van shot forward onto the street. The screech of tires from the SUV and van was deafening as the van slid to a stop followed by the SUV, which stopped three feet away. Jake was out of the van before it fully stopped, his gun pointed at the driver. Sword hopped out the driver's side and raced to where the SUV was now idling, his weapon drawn and ready to use.

"Get out of the car!" shouted Jake, moving a step closer. He was just two feet from the SUV and could clearly see the driver's face. "Get out of the car now!" The driver suddenly threw the car in reverse and hit the gas. Before it had moved two feet, Jake pumped two bullets into the hood and one into the front tire. Smoke billowed up from the hood as the SUV rolled to a stop. "Last warning, get the fuck out of the car!"

The driver opened his door. "I alone. No speak good English."

"Bullshit!" Jake growled. "We know there's someone in the back. Both of you, get out now!"

Sword rushed behind Jake to the passenger door. Quickly pointing his weapon at the back window of the SUV on the passenger side, he fired a shot. The window disintegrated and shards of glass flew inside the vehicle and outside to the ground.

The passenger door flew open. "Okay, okay, no shoot."

"Show me your hands!" shouted Jake. "Quiero ver tus manos!"

The man in back shoved his hands out the door. In one swoop, Sword reached in and grabbed his hands with one of his own, yanking him out of the vehicle and tossing him on the ground like a slab of beef. "Don't move."

Jake still had his eyes on the driver, who had not moved. When Jake observed the driver's eyes flicking down, he didn't hesitate. The bullet hit the driver between the eyes and exploded out the back of his head. Blood and brain tissue splattered across the dashboard. Jake walked up to the driver's door and glanced down, noting the gun in the driver's hand.

"Good call, Pirate." Sword peeked inside. "Nice shot too. What do you want to do with him?" He pointed to the man lying on the ground.

"Cenzo." Jake shook his head. "Damn." He sighed. "Tie him up and toss him in the back of the van. We need to split. Who knows if he had time to call anyone at Systap. Head further north on ninety-five. Let's find a quiet, remote place to have a chat."

Sword motioned for Cenzo to stand then tied his hands behind him and shoved him into the back of the van. Before closing the door, Sword also tied his ankles together then pushed him down, forcing him to lie on his side.

"What do you want from me? I'm just a factory worker, heading home after a long day of work. And who is this Cenzo person?"

Jake laughed and turned in his seat to look back at Cenzo. "I hope you're comfortable back there, although being tied up like a hog doesn't look particularly pleasant." He laughed again. "Must be good pay for a factory worker to have a top-of-the-line SUV with a personal driver."

Sword laughed too. "Maybe I need to look into that line of work."

"Cut the bullshit, Cenzo." Jake's voice turned to ice,

the words cutting and harsh. "We know who you are and that you work for Armano and the Los Rinches cartel. And you were the one who recognized me in Cabo. I want some answers and you're going to give them to me."

Cenzo clamped his mouth shut and turned his head away.

"Suit yourself. You'll talk as soon as we stop." Jake faced forward again. "Take the next exit. There's a road up ahead to the right that has possibilities."

Ten minutes later, Sword pulled the van to the side of the dirt road they were on. They were out of sight of ninety-five and near a large outcropping of rocks. Sword and Jake got out of the van and walked to the back, throwing open the rear doors. Sword reached in and pulled Cenzo out by his legs. His head hit the bumper as he bounced out. Since his arms were tied behind his back, nothing broke his fall and he landed on his shoulder before his face hit the hard dirt.

Cenzo groaned.

"On your feet." Sword cut the ties holding his ankles then yanked him up by his arms.

Cenzo coughed, spitting out blood and a couple of teeth. "You'll pay for this," he managed to say, blood and saliva dribbling down his chin.

"Move it." Sword shoved him in the back, causing Cenzo to stumble. As they walked to the rocks, he alternately complained and threatened them with every step he took. When they reached the largest rock, Sword pushed him up against it.

"Tell me about the candy app operation. Who was with you and Armano? Does he run the operation here? Are there other properties like this one? Who makes the fentanyl? How is the candy delivered?" Jake rattled off multiple questions.

Despite his circumstances, Cenzo looked Jake up and down. His lip curled up. "So many questions, and you think I know the answers?" he snarled. "Now that is funny." He wasn't laughing. "Or should I say," and he altered his voice to sound like Jake, "Hi Dad. Just wanted to let you know that we sent you a little something from Cabo. It may melt so open it right away. We hope you and Heather enjoy it." His laugh sounded coarse and evil. Speaking in his own voice, he asked. "Did they enjoy the candy?"

Jake's eyes flashed and he saw red. "You son-of-a-bitch." He stepped forward and slammed his fist into Cenzo's stomach, causing him to double over in pain. When Jake moved to hit him again, Sword grabbed his arm. Jake turned furious eyes on him.

"We need answers, Pirate."

Jake shook off Sword's arm then turned and walked away, breathing heavily. When he felt like he was in control, he walked back to Cenzo, who was standing upright again, although he was rubbing his stomach and his body tilted to the side a little.

"Who was with you and Armano, and does he run the operation here? And what's your role?"

Cenzo coughed. "You know my role. As for Mojado..."

They all stopped and looked up when they heard a buzzing sound that was growing louder.

"What the hell?" Sword pointed toward ninety-five.

Cenzo giggled. "I said you'd pay, pendejo."

"It's a drone," said Jake. "He must have called before he got out of the SUV."

"Hijole! Much simpler than that. Everyone who works for Armano has a tracking device inserted in their arm." He pointed to his bicep. "Armano always knows where his people are."

"That's a rifle barrel hanging from the bottom." Sword's eyes shot to Jake, who was still staring at the drone.

Before they took their next breath, the pop, pop of a gun could be heard. They instinctively ducked.

"We can't stay here, we're sitting ducks with that thing," said Jake. "To the van on the count of three." He paused, watching the drone. "Three!"

Sword grabbed Cenzo and pulled him behind him as he raced toward the van. Jake ran alongside, taking shots at the drone, trying to bring it down. As the drone drew closer, Jake and Sword both tried to shoot it down, causing it to break off and circle behind them. As they reached the van, they heard the pop of a shot fired. It hit Cenzo squarely in the back. Gasping, he went down, almost pulling Sword down with him. Jake turned and fired three more rapid shots then jumped into the passenger seat. The drone fired twice more, hitting the side of the van, then moved up and over the van, too high for the series of shots Sword got off as he yanked open his door. Dropping down, the drone shot twice more, hitting Sword in his left leg. Jake opened the door and stood on the floorboard. Turning, he raised his gun over the hood of the van and fired one shot, hitting the drone as it was moving closer to take another shot at Sword. A popping sound came from the drone then it dropped to the ground.

"Can you drive?" he asked Sword.

Gritting his teeth, Sword said, "Yes, the bullet only grazed my thigh."

"We need to get the hell out of here. Armano's men probably aren't far behind that drone."

Sword jammed the van into drive and floored it. They shot down the dusty road.

"Are you guys okay?" Mali asked, concern evident in her voice. Since the comm line was open, she and Kirsten had heard the entire exchange.

At the same time, Felix shouted, "Hey, Matey just said he was about to be taken. He tossed his Bluetooth."

"Oh God," said Kirsten.

Two trucks turned onto the road and sped toward Jake and Sword.

"We're about to be taken too. Felix, get back to the ranch. Hoop, the third man, the man in the hoodie, is Jeff. Mojado, the term Cenzo used, is slang for Slick. Contact Angela. We're tossing our Bluetooths."

"Jake! Jake!"

There was no response.

CHAPTER TWENTY-ONE

THIRTY MINUTES LATER, Jake and Sword were escorted onto the property. As they passed through the inner gate and neared the three buildings, they noticed what looked like multiple barracks to the left and down a hill. They had not seen them in the video Jeff sent. *Not surprising*, thought Jake, *Jeff was obviously careful what he allowed us to see.*

The trucks parked next to building one and they were taken inside. It was different from the plans they reviewed back at the ranch. There were two levels. The upper level only encompassed half the length of the building and it was open to the floor below. The main level housed all the candy and it was well organized, with the candy categorized alphabetically in row after row. There were no offices on this level.

"Pirate, old friend. And, my God, is that Sword? How the hell are you?" Jeff called out, as he approached them.

Jake lunged at him but was quickly grabbed from behind and held back. "You son-of-a-bitch! You killed my dad and could have killed Heather!"

Jeff shrugged, lifting hands open and wide waist-high. "Collateral damage, unfortunately. Armano told me how his father was killed in a raid, but I never connected it to you. I knew you worked that region of Mexico but assumed you had left the Army already. Another team was sent in after you and I was under the impression that they took out Armano senior. When Cenzo recognized you on your honeymoon, Armano sent me your picture asking me to locate you. Talk about a coincidence, we were already working together." He laughed a big belly laugh, grabbing his midsection as he did so. "Damn shame we had to kill Cenzo, though. He had unique skills." He shrugged again, shaking his head. "Such is life."

"You bastard," said Sword.

"Hey, that's no way to talk to an old Army pal." He chuckled. "Come, let me show you the place before we head upstairs." Jeff led them down row after row of candy, passing multiple workers. They worked in pairs, one walking on the ground, another on stilts, grabbing candy high and low to fill the orders. The worker on stilts dropped the candy to the worker walking alongside him.

Seeing their curiosity, Jeff said, "They work in pairs to keep things moving along. When an order is filled, they take the basket of candy over there," he pointed to the other end of the warehouse, "and a team boxes it up. Each individual order is sorted according to state then city and placed in larger containers accordingly. The eighteen-wheelers take the candy to smaller distribution centers in each state. We have three drivers per truck, and they can drive straight through. Most distribution centers are relatively small, depending on the demand. The distribution center in North Dakota, yes, there's demand even there, is someone's house. Crazy, right? Who knew candy could be so popular?"

"Yeah, especially when laced with drugs," growled Jake. "How the hell did you get involved in this, Slick? Why?"

"I'll give you twenty thousand reasons why, and that's per month, all cash, non-taxable. I saw an opportunity in Mexico, when we were doing our counter drug operations, and took it. While there, we destroyed some agreed upon smaller labs, to keep the Army colonels happy." He grinned. "All the while, I started working on a more extensive distribution network for what would become Armano's candy operation. Even then, he knew the path that would lead to success, despite not knowing exactly how to get there at the time. He has a brilliant mind, honed to perfection as he grew up."

"You admire him? He has killed thousands of innocent people, and now children, with his poison, and–"

Raising his hand to stop him, Jeff said, "Damn right I do! So spare me the outrage, Pirate. No one forces people to snort cocaine or to shoot up. Supply and demand, baby."

"What about those who accidentally eat the fentanyl-laced candy, like those nine-year-old boys in Colorado last month when the boy's mother used an obviously flawed candy app and ordered the wrong stuff?

Or the veterans, just a few days ago, when some sick kids decided to play a game that the vets didn't even know they were playing?" Jake smirked. "I bet you created the app, right?"

Jeff's lips thinned and he stopped to glare at Jake. "The candy app may need a few minor tweaks but it's a masterpiece." His chest rising and falling rapidly, Jeff spun around and walked a few paces away. Hands on hips, his eyes were fixated on the candy on the shelves.

Finally, he turned back, smile in place and continued his story as if the exchange between Jake and himself never occurred. "When I resigned my commission, I joined the FBI like you because, well, what better place to continue building the network while keeping tabs on things our government was doing. Our network is now the largest in the country and will soon be the largest in the world." His chest puffed up with pride. "I was going to join the DEA but decided against it, too easy to get caught. They are much smarter than FBI pukes, present company excepted of course." His belly laugh rose to the rafters.

Approaching the stairs, Jeff led them up without further comment. They walked down a long hallway on a floor that was made of metal grates. Looking down, you could look through to the floor below. One side of the hall was open to the floor, with a handrail, and the other side was a series of rooms. Walking to the last room, Jeff pulled out a set of keys and opened the door. Stepping aside, the two men walking behind Jake and Sword shoved them inside.

"I've got work that needs my attention. We'll talk more later." Jeff closed the door behind him, and they heard the key turn, locking them in.

"Christ!" Sword looked to his right. Matey was lying on his side on the floor, knees curled up toward his chest. He was unconscious, his face was bruised, and he had a bloody nose and lip. Sword and Jake rushed over to him, Sword reaching him first.

"Is he alive?" asked Jake.

* * *

Nevada ranch
Tuesday, January 18, 6:30 a.m.

"I'm sorry I couldn't get here sooner. I didn't even hear your message until after midnight last night." She studied their base of operations, nodding in appreciation. "When did you arrive?"

Mali hugged her, motioned with her arm to precede her, then they walked to the dining table. "Sunday night. I'm sorry we didn't call sooner but things moved very fast the moment we returned to Scranton, and Jake's plan started within two hours of our arrival. Time got away from us." Feeling Kirsten's eyes boring into her, Mali glanced at her and gave a little shake of her head. She made quick introductions as Kirsten joined them at the table.

Angela placed her hand on Mali's arm. "First of all, are you okay?"

"Last night, I was pretty frantic. I hardly slept at

all. I don't think Jeff or Armano will rush to kill them, though, so I'm calmer."

"Tell me exactly what happened."

Mali and Kirsten stepped through the series of events from the time the recon began until the moment Jake told them he was being taken the previous night.

"So you've confirmed the Systap property is their distribution center, and they actually make the fentanyl on site?"

Mali nodded.

"Unbelievable. I agree that they probably haven't killed Jake or the other two at this point."

"So let's call your office, get in there and kick butt," said Kirsten.

"I called them while I was driving here. They're putting a team together and should be contacting me with a plan."

Kirsten excused herself, saying she needed to check a few things on her laptop. She walked to the kitchen island and was soon focused on the screen.

Do you have any weapons?" Angela asked, looking around.

"Yes, Sword brought a variety." They walked to the hearth where Sword had laid out most of them.

Whistling, Angela picked up a rifle. "Wow! An MD-15, standard AR15 style, short barrel with reduced recoil. I haven't seen one of these since training." She set it down and smiled at Mali. "I went through an extended weapons training program last year. We learned about all types of weapons, standard weapons the FBI uses as well as non-standard weapons. I even got to shoot a cross-bow a few times."

"This is most of what Sword brought. They carried a few weapons for their recon mission but didn't expect to engage. They just wanted to observe. The plans changed on the fly when Jake recognized Armano."

"Adapting to the situation." Angela nodded. "That's why Jake–"

"Hey Hoop." Felix walked in, looking down at the laptop he held. "I went over some video I missed last night…" His voice trailed off when he looked up and saw Angela standing next to Mali.

"Felix, this is Agent Angela Whitby. She just arrived to help. Angela, Felix is one of our technical wizards."

Felix snapped his laptop shut. His eyes flicked from Angela to Mali and back. Stepping over to them, he shook Angela's hand, mumbling hello. He glanced at Mali and said, "I'm sorry to be late getting out here. That shower felt too good. When you have time, I have stuff to show you. I'm going to grab some coffee." He turned and hurried over to the kitchen.

Mali followed his progress, a quizzical look on her face, before turning back to Angela. "I'm sorry. I didn't even offer you coffee or something to eat."

"Coffee sounds perfect. I didn't stop for any on my way over here and I'm dying." She smiled. "But first, can you point me in the direction of the bathroom?"

"Of course. It's just down the hall to the left."

"Thanks." She disappeared around the corner.

Mali walked into the kitchen and joined Felix and

Kirsten, who were hovering over his laptop and whispering furiously.

"When Agent Whitby didn't return your call last night, I figured she wasn't coming," said Felix. Mali had to lean in to hear him.

"There was no need. Following my phone call, I texted her the address telling her to come as soon as she could." She looked from Felix to Kirsten. "What's going on?"

"I started to tell you. I set up a little program, incorporating the satellite, to record when Agent Whitby went somewhere in her car, you know, if I was in the john or something. After my shower just now, I checked and realized that I missed two recordings late last night. Look where she went at ten-forty-five. She didn't return to her home until twelve-fifteen this morning."

He flipped his laptop around. "This is the first video. It's the interesting one. I already clicked the link for the details."

"Okay, she's parked at a restaurant of some sort?"

"It's called the Stonehouse Bar & Grill, located in North Las Vegas," he replied, as he and Kirsten skirted the island to watch the video with her.

"Felix…"

"I set it up so that the system keeps recording for thirty seconds after she parks. Keep watching."

Fifteen seconds later, a truck pulls in and parks next to Angela's car. Just before the recording stopped, they watched Jeff step out of the truck.

Mali frowned.

"Well, it looks like the cat's out of the bag," a voice snickered in front of them.

Three pairs of eyes flew up from the screen in surprise.

Angela was standing by the dining table, pointing a Glock .45 at them.

"I have to say that I'm impressed. I didn't realize you had placed a tracker on my car. Good one." She cackled.

"Angela…"

"Oh, spare me, Mali," she sneered. "You have no idea how lucky you are to have found a man who loves you. It's not easy meeting quality men here in Vegas. The morons I work with are not anyone I'd ever consider dating. Then I met Jeff when I helped all of you a few months ago. He wasn't with Jake, of course, when we followed you and that bitch to Lake Tahoe. But we started video chatting afterward. One thing led to another and when he came here, we connected." She giggled. "He is amazing. A few weeks ago, he trusted me enough to tell me about the operation and his role in it. That blew me away, and I realized just how much he loves me. He's offered me the world and I'm taking it." She glared at Mali. "Then you and Jake came and wanted to ruin things."

"Angela, they killed Jake's dad. They could have killed his seven-year-old daughter, Heather, if she had been home when the candy arrived."

Angela sighed. "That's a shame, but Jeff said it couldn't be helped. Be glad Heather was gone." She nodded toward the door with her head. "Time to go."

Mali, Kirsten, and Felix were all standing behind the kitchen island, the open laptop in front of them. Gesturing behind the island for them to go the other way, Mali took one small step to her left, then another, while Felix and Kirsten inched to the right. They were putting space between each other.

"That's far enough. You don't think I know what you're trying to do?" Her voice rose with each word. She fired a shot at the cabinet above Mali's head. The sound of the gun and the wood splintering above their heads surprised them and they all instinctively ducked below the island.

Mali scrambled to the left side on her hands and knees, yelling at Angela not to shoot, hoping to distract her for a few seconds. If Kirsten and Felix could get beyond the corner and down the hall, they might be able to get away.

Angela was closest to Mali's side of the kitchen and rushed past the dining table to get to her.

"Hold it right there." Mali looked up from her crouched position and stared up the barrel of Angela's gun. She saw Angela glance up, raise her gun, and fire a shot. Kirsten screamed. When Mali looked over her shoulder, she saw Kirsten grab her leg as Felix dragged her around the corner.

Mali jumped up, putting herself in the line of fire. "Leave them. It's me you want."

Angela's eyes shifted to Mali as did her gun. She nodded. "They won't be able to help you, anyway. Grab their phones and let's go." Mali did as she was told, not mentioning that there were more burner phones in Sword's other duffel bag, and picked up her purse that was sitting on the table by the door. When they walked outside, Angela shot the tires on the passenger side of their vehicle.

"You drive," she said, nudging Mali to the driver's side of her Jeep. "And don't try anything stupid. I don't want to shoot you, but I will if I have to."

CHAPTER TWENTY-TWO

Systap property
Tuesday, January 18, 8:25 a.m.

THE DRIVE WAS mostly made in silence. Mali initially tried to engage Angela in conversation to convince her, in some way, to stop what she was doing and help them. When Angela reached over to turn on the radio, Mali subsided into silence. She followed Angela's non-verbal gestures without question and used the time to figure out ways to help Jake and the others when she arrived. She hoped they had a plan. Thinking of how they would get out of their situation alive was better than thinking of how dire their situation actually was. It was a long drive.

As they approached the outer gate, Angela unzipped the fanny pack at her waist with her free hand and reached in, pulling the green identity badge out. Finally speaking to Mali, she instructed her to lower the window. The guard walked over and leaned down, looking inside. He glanced first at Mali then at Angela. When he noticed her gun, now lying in her lap, he raised his rifle to his waist in a ready position. Mali tensed, seeing only her reflection in the mirrors of his aviator sunglasses, and leaned back as far as the seat would allow. He lowered it after studying the badge he grabbed from Angela's extended hand. Sniffing, he handed the badge back through the window and gestured with his rifle to enter.

Angela chuckled. "Oooops!" She placed her weapon under the passenger's front seat as they drove up to the inner gate. Showing her badge to the next guard, she asked him for the location of Armano and Jeff. She was directed to the barracks on the far side of the compound.

Mali observed the rows of barracks to the left, slightly down the hill, as they passed buildings one and two. She slowed down to allow two workers to cross from the barracks to building two, then observed others walking between the two buildings pushing what appeared to be carts full of boxes. Mali drove by building three, which she noticed had no windows and the workers who entered wore full hazmat gear. At the end of building three, the dirt road curved to the left and sloped down.

"Pull in next to the truck at the barracks on the right."

Mali did as instructed, then turned the engine off. They both exited the vehicle and Angela rounded the back, grabbing Mali by her elbow and walking with her to the metal door. Opening it, she shoved Mali inside and closed the door behind her. Despite the fact that a row of fluorescent lights running the length of the ceiling were on, it took a moment for Mali's eyes to adjust after the brightness of the sun outside. This room was evidently used for supplies of sorts. Stacks upon stacks of varying sizes of folded brown boxes—four, five, and even six feet high—were on the right side and ran the length of the room. On the left side, rows of metal shelving held masks, surgical gloves, rubber boots, and other various hazmat gear as well as packing tape, mailing labels, and some items that were undistinguishable. The middle of the barracks was a walkway they now traversed. The back end of the room contained metal tables and benches.

Mali's breath caught when she saw Jake, Sword, and Matey. Jake and Sword appeared unharmed, but Matey was lying on his back on one of the benches.

"You're late." Jeff grumbled, as he walked up to Angela.

Releasing Mali's elbow, she said, "Couldn't be helped. Ran into a little problem, but I took care of it." She smiled the smile of a smitten high school girl, grabbed his waist, and leaned in for a kiss.

Pulling her close, he obliged her, extending the kiss and squeezing her butt with his hands as he held her. "Mmmm, that's more like it," he murmured.

As soon as Angela released her, Mali had rushed over to Jake.

Ignoring the two guards behind them, he stood and wrapped her in a bear hug. "Are you okay?" he asked.

Mali nodded, tears in her eyes. "I've been worried about you." She pulled away and turned toward Sword, noticing his leg for the first time. "Your leg!"

"Just a scratch."

Mali nodded then looked at Matey with concern.

"He was beaten pretty bad but he's holding on," said Sword to her unasked question.

"I'm still alive," mumbled Matey when he heard what Sword said.

"Hoop, it's good to see you," said Jeff. He was holding Angela's hand and they were standing two tables away. "We've been waiting for you."

She glared at him but stayed silent. Jake moved Mali slightly behind him.

Noticing that, Jeff laughed. "So protective." He looked from one to the other. "You might as well relax for a bit. Armano had some business to attend to. We'll just sit and wait for him." Jeff paused, fists clenching. "He's looking forward to this, Pirate. So am I." Angela was leaning against the table and Jeff turned to her, dismissing the team and speaking to her in low tones.

Jake squeezed Mali's hand. "Felix and Kirsten?"

"Angela shot Kirsten in the leg, but Felix was able to pull her out of the line of additional fire. They're still at the ranch."

Jeff was instantly on alert, eyes bulging as he pulled back from Angela and stared into her face. "They're still alive?" The words boomed from deep in his belly.

Angela shrunk back, trembling. "I...I..."

Jeff backhanded her, sending her flying to the floor.

Crying, and with one hand on her bloody mouth, she rolled over. Pushing herself up to her knees, she looked up at Jeff, tears rolling down her cheeks. "She was injured and I took their phones. I shot the tires of their car before we left. There's nothing they can do."

Sensing an opportunity, Mali offered, "Actually, there are more burner phones in Sword's duffel bag that Angela didn't look through. They've probably called the cops already."

Jeff had turned his head toward Mali as she spoke. When she finished, Jeff's eyes filled with rage and he turned back to Angela. "You stupid bitch." Pulling his gun out of his holster, he fired one shot, hitting her in the head. It happened so fast, she didn't have a chance to react. Her body fell back, and a pool of blood began to gather under what was left of her head.

"Oh God." Mali turned her head into Jake's shoulder. "I didn't think he'd kill her," she whispered.

Still fuming, Jeff shouted at the guards. "Keep your eyes on them. If they try anything, kill them." He turned and stomped down the hall, his boots echoing in the room, then slammed out the barracks door.

* * *

Jake shifted positions, his back now to the two guards, and glanced at Sword. Mali noticed the look that passed between them. Leaning his head down, he kissed her forehead and whispered, "Try to go to the bathroom."

Mali pretended to whisper to Jake.

"No talking." One of the guards shook his head when Mali looked up at him.

"I was telling my husband that I need to use the restroom."

He appeared to be Hispanic, but he obviously

understood what she said. Looking down his nose at her, he smiled and again shook his head.

"You don't understand. Angela took me out of the house so fast, I didn't have a chance to use it. At this point, I'm about to explode. Please," she beseeched, and hoped the look she gave him was one of desperation. She began to wiggle in her seat. "Look at me. I'm not in a position to do anything and, really, do I look like I could hurt a big fella like you?"

The guard she spoke to turned to the other guard, who said, "Mojado said no move."

Mali glared at each guard. "I realize that. But I'm about to pee my pants and, believe me, that will not be a pretty picture. Please, please let me use it," she implored.

The first guard rolled his eyes in exasperation, as if to say 'women.' With his rifle, he motioned for her to stand up and pointed to the door a few yards away at the back of the room. When she stood and made a move to walk past him, he turned his weapon toward her. She was standing close enough to him that the middle section of his rifle touched her midriff and she could smell his rank breath.

"No funny business. Leave purse." Without taking her eyes off him, she dropped her purse onto the bench. It landed with a clunk. Mali didn't waste any time and headed straight to the door he indicated. Opening it, she noted the rudimentary bathroom. It wasn't much bigger than a coat closet and held a small sink on a pedestal with a toilet opposite it.

She was just stepping inside when she heard a scuffle

behind her and some grunts followed by the clanking of metal hitting the ground. Looking back, her eyebrows shot up. She watched as the first guard fell straight back, like a tree toppling, rifle still in his arms. Sword squatted next to him, searched him for ammunition then picked up the rifle. At the same time the first guard was falling, Jake was punching the second guard in the nose, his rifle already on the ground. Nose bloodied, the guard responded with a right hook, the blow glancing off Jake's chin.

They continued to trade blows as Mali made her way cautiously back to the tables. Sword sidled around the two who were fighting and picked up the second rifle. Making his way back to Mali, who was standing next to the bench by her purse, he grinned and set one rifle on the table next to her, before taking a defensive stance with the first rifle, ready to act if needed.

"Aren't you going to help?" she asked, automatically slipping her purse over her shoulder so it crossed her body.

"Nope."

She sighed and shook her head. *Men!*

Just when it looked like Jake had the upper hand, the guard managed to pull the revolver from the holster at his waist.

"Gun!" Sword yanked Mali behind him. Jake used his left arm to deflect the weapon as it discharged. With the guard's arm up, his midsection was exposed. Jake punched him in his stomach and when he doubled over, thrust his knee into the guard's chin. The force threw the man's head up and back. He landed flat on his back, out cold.

Jake bent over and breathed deeply for a few seconds. Reaching over the guard, he picked up the revolver then turned toward Sword and Mali.

"You're getting soft," said Sword, chuckling.

"Go to hell." But Jake was smiling.

Mali peeked beyond Sword and saw that Jake's shoulder was bleeding. Gasping, she pushed Sword out of the way and rushed to Jake. "You were shot."

He looked down at his shoulder. "Barely a scrape."

Sword said, "They'll be coming."

Jake nodded, picked up the rifle that was on the table, and walked over to Matey. Leaning down, he asked, "How're you doing?"

Matey turned his head, opening his one good eye. "I'll live, although I'll feel a hell of a lot better when we're out of here."

"Agreed. There's a side door back here. Let's go."

As Sword helped Matey up, loud shouting preceded the barracks door flying open. Matey groaned when Sword dropped him on the ground then flipped a metal table on its side, the table now acting as a barrier. Matey lay on his side behind Sword. Jake did the same to the table next to Sword, shoving Mali down and behind him.

Four guards flew down the hall toward the back with Jeff behind them. Shots from the two front guards hit the table and others flew high, before Sword and Jake took them out with one single bullet each. As they fell, the other two guards and Jeff took cover behind the mountains of boxes on one side and the metal shelving on the other.

Bullets pinged the metal table making loud popping noises, and men were shouting back and forth to each other. The cacophony of noise was deafening. Mali covered her ears as she crouched behind Jake.

"How much ammo do you have?" shouted Jake.

"Not enough, maybe half a clip," was Sword's response. He peeked over the top and fired another round. "The guard wasn't carrying extra clips, probably never expected trouble."

Jake's lips thinned as he looked around. "Pull the tables with us and move toward the back door. Maybe we can get outside before they circle us."

They began to inch their way backward, Matey and Mali scooting a few inches followed by Sword and Jake with the tables in front of them. They each pulled the table from the lip with one hand while keeping watch in front of them, shooting occasionally to force Jeff and the guards to remain behind cover. The effort was painstakingly slow.

They had pulled back roughly two feet when the shooting stopped.

Jeff called out. "You have nowhere to go, Pirate. More guards have joined me. You're outnumbered. Give it up and you might avoid suffering."

Glancing to her side, Mali watched Matey look to his left then signal Jake for the gun. Jake slid it to him, and in one motion, he picked it up and swung his arm to the side, shooting a guard who was creeping to the far side of the nearest stack of boxes.

That started another round of shooting from the guards before a shrill whistle sounded behind them. The shooting ceased once more.

Mali was just turning her head to look behind her when there was a rush of air at her back and she was grabbed from behind. She screamed as a strong arm yanked her up, and her body slammed into an equally muscular body.

Jake turned his head, immediately dropping the rifle he held. He spun and rose from his crouched position in one fluid motion. "Armano."

CHAPTER TWENTY-THREE

SWORD AND MATEY dropped their weapons as well, Sword helping Matey up to stand next to Jake.

"A wise move, Pirate. That is what your friend, my compadre, calls you, yes?" Dressed in jeans and a loose white shirt, a barefoot Armano was positioned behind Mali. One arm was around her waist, his other arm was raised and he held a syringe in his hand next to her neck.

Mali was breathing rapidly with short breaths, her wide eyes fixed on Jake. Her arms were crossed at her waist, one on top of the other, Armano's arm was over both as he held her tight.

"Let her go, Armano. It's me you want."

He chuckled, waving the syringe around. "Where would the fun be in that? I'm sure you realize by now that the syringe is full of fentanyl. Less than one drop would kill her muy rapidamente."

Jeff and three guards joined Armano. The guards seemed to be fascinated as Jeff grinned.

"Wait!" Jake called out, raising his arm out in front of him. He shifted slightly sideways, as if to step over the weapons on the ground.

Jeff raised his weapon and shook his head.

"Not to worry," Armano cajoled. "I am not ready to end the life of your lovely wife just yet. We have a little time."

Mali tried to calm down so she could think, slowing her breathing and inhaling deeply while holding very still. The needle wasn't touching her but she could sense how close it was. Shifting her focus, her eyes fell on the two guards who were standing behind Jake and Sword. She frowned, allowing her eyes to dart from left to right, searching. There were no other guards behind them. Returning her gaze to Jake, she slowly bent the pinky and ring fingers of her left hand and tucked her thumb under her palm, leaving her forefinger and middle finger exposed and open. His eyes continually roamed the room and it took her a moment to catch his attention. When he finally looked at her, she flicked hers down toward her fingers then to the guards behind Jake and hoped he'd get the message. She watched him continue to move his eyes, first staring at Jeff, then the guards and Armano. When he glanced down at her fingers again and his eyes meandered up to hers, she knew he got the message.

"Imagine my surprise when Cenzo contacted me telling me that the man who killed my father was actually alive and enjoying time in Cabo. I was sure you had died back in Mexico all those years ago. Dios mio! You were shot four or five times! You must have nine lives, no?" He sobered, glaring at Jake. "Mi madre and I buried my father and two sisters, and I moved on with my life, mi madre with me, although she is a shell of her former self because of what you did." His brow cleared and his mood lightened once again. "Now look at the empire I have built. Though he was my father and I loved him, he was weak in many ways. He was not willing to take our organization to the next level, where it needed to go. Fentanyl is the future. It is cheap to make and, when mixed with coca or other delectables you Americans crave, people get a more exhilarating high and want more. Of course, the reality is that they want more fentanyl not the coca, which only makes me richer." He laughed.

Mali's hands fisted as she listened to him speak, anger making for loose lips. "You are killing innocent children with your candy, children by the way, who do not want drugs of any kind," she spat, lips thinned, body rigid. "But your app is getting too much notice now. When the authorities realize how the illegal drugs are ordered and that you're making fentanyl on U.S. soil, your empire will crumble."

He dropped the arm holding the syringe to lean around her and look down into defiant eyes. "You are a feisty one." He straightened and looked back at Jake. "I—"

Two things happened in the next instant. Matey crumpled to the ground and Mali raised her right foot slamming the block heel of her beige ankle bootie down on Armano's bare foot.

Chaos erupted.

Armano howled in pain, releasing Mali. As she

started to pull away, Armano swung the arm that was holding the syringe, nicking her upper arm. She cried out as Jake leapt forward, pushing her out of the way and slamming his body into Armano. The syringe flew out of his hand as both men went down.

"Use the Narcan," he shouted.

At the same time, Matey, now on the ground, picked up the revolver he had set down earlier and shot Jeff, while Sword leaned over and pulled two white Ninja stars from his boot. Twisting around, he threw the stars at the two guards behind them. Blood began to trail down their chests from where the stars were sticking out of their necks. Gurgling, their hands moved to their throats, before both men dropped to the ground.

The three guards who were beside Armano and Jeff, seemed stunned and it took them a moment to react. By then, it was too late. Sword picked up the rifle from the ground and shot all three.

As Jake and Armano struggled, Mali fumbled with her purse that was still crossed over her chest, trying to open it. Sitting on the floor where she landed after Jake pushed her, she blinked a few times, trying to focus, swaying slightly from side to side. The thought crossed her mind that she might throw up.

Rushing over to her, Sword kneeled down and grabbed her purse from her hands. He opened it and pulled out the cylinder. Popping the lid, he extracted one Narcan pen and jammed it into her thigh.

"Ow," she said, trying to lift her head to look at him but it was too heavy.

"Lie back," he said. Supporting her neck, he pushed her gently back until she was lying flat on her back. He administered the second dose of Narcan. "Don't move."

The last thing Mali heard was gunfire in the distance.

* * *

After Jake slammed into Armano, they both hit the floor. The syringe flew out of Armano's hand and skidded to a stop next to a bench. Rolling on top of Jake, Armano half-sat on him, punching him twice in the face. Grunting, Jake grabbed Armano's shoulders and used his hips and legs to thrust up and throw him over his head. Springing up, he pivoted and kicked Armano in the stomach as he was gaining his feet. Armano went down on one knee and quickly searched the floor. Jake eyed the syringe the same time Armano did. Both dove for it but Armano was closer. He grabbed the syringe and jumped up to face Jake, who had scrambled to his feet. They began to circle each other.

"Not bad, gringo, although you didn't touch my pretty face. I messed yours up pretty good." Armano chortled, waving the syringe in front of him.

Crouched low and hands spread wide and to his sides, Jake said, "I'm saving the best for last." He spit blood out of his mouth, never taking his eyes off Armano. "You're about to get a taste of your own medicine before I bring your organization down."

"Waaaaaahhhhhh. Waaaaaahhhhhh."

Jake noticed that the gun fire had ceased and he just heard sirens now. "Hear that, you scum? The authorities are pulling in and your time is up." His lips curled upward.

Armano cocked his head to the side, his eyes widening before they lowered into a frown. "Pendejo," he screamed. Eyes wild, he charged Jake, the hand holding the syringe high in the air.

Jake reached up and grabbed that arm, while sidestepping him, and twisted it behind him. Now standing behind Armano, he wrenched the syringe out of his hand and plunged it into his neck, dispensing the fentanyl before pushing Armano away, syringe still stuck there.

Armano staggered back a few steps, gasping, before dropping to the floor on his knees. Eyes wide, he fell to his side, hand still on the syringe. Jake backed away, watching Armano's lips turn blue as he vomited repeatedly. His body stiffened and jerked a few times before his breathing slowed then stopped altogether. He was dead in less than a minute.

Turning from him, Jake rushed over to Mali. He pushed Sword aside and kneeled next to her. "How is she?"

"Her skin was a little clammy and breathing had slowed before I gave her both doses. She's breathing normally now and her skin feels fine."

"Thank God." He choked out, brushing the hair off her face. He cleared his throat. "We need to get out of here and we'll all need Narcan, just to be safe."

"I feel just fine," mumbled Matey. "Ready to rumble."

Sword and Jake shook their heads and chuckled.

Then Jake leaned down and picked Mali up while Sword helped Matey stand.

When Jake heard Mali moan, he looked down. "Welcome back." He kissed her forehead.

"It's over?"

He nodded. "Armano and Jeff are dead."

"Sword and Matey?" She looked around.

"We're right here," said Sword.

Mali smiled in relief then looked up at Jake. "I can walk."

He shook his head. "I like having you right here." He pulled her even closer.

Sighing, she laid her head on his shoulder and closed her eyes.

They cautiously made their way to the front of the building. They weren't sure what they would find outside so Sword led the way, a rifle in his arms. He opened the door an inch and looked through the opening with his eye. After scanning left and right, he leaned back and glanced at the others over his shoulder. "The place is swarming with the Feds and DEA." Pushing the door all the way open, he laid the rifle next to it and the four stepped outside. They were immediately surrounded.

CHAPTER TWENTY-FOUR

THE TEAM HAD been moved to building one. Mali and Matey were sitting outside on chairs that had been moved from inside, and EMS was checking them out. Both would soon to be transported to the hospital by ambulance. They suspected that Matey had three broken ribs on his left side and a couple on the right. There was no evidence of internal bleeding, but he would have to be checked nonetheless. Mali needed to be assessed after her exposure to the fentanyl, and to ensure she suffered no ill effects from the Naloxone.

Jake and Sword were given doses of Narcan and would also go to the hospital to tend to their wounds. They were standing to the side briefing the DEA agent-in-charge.

DEA and federal agents were everywhere, interviewing workers, conducting an inventory of product, and moving prisoners to a makeshift pen close to the inner gate. Two agents guarded them as others continued to round them up. It was going to take a long time to wrap up the case.

Mali watched a black sedan pull up and smiled when Felix and Kirsten stepped out of the vehicle.

"You guys look like crap," Felix said as he made his way to the team, Kirsten limping right behind him.

Jake, Sword, and the agent-in-charge joined the group. A local FBI agent also joined them.

"You and Kirsten don't look much better," said Sword, slapping Felix on the back.

"We were so worried," said Kirsten, as she leaned down to hug Mali. "After Agent Whitby took you, Felix wrapped my leg and found one of the burner phones. He called the local FBI office and explained what was going on. We couldn't go anywhere because of the car, but they sent an ambulance and then met us at the hospital." She lifted her bandaged leg. "The doctor said the bullet went straight through, didn't hit any bones."

"That's good news. Are you in pain?"

"It stings but they gave me Percocet to take the edge off. The agents brought us straight here after the hospital released me."

Felix whistled as he checked out his surroundings. "Quite an operation here. What happened, and what about Agent Whitby?"

"Angela is dead, shot by Jeff," said Mali. Explaining for the benefit of the two agents, she added, "She told us at the ranch that she connected with Jeff after the Janet Simpson case. He eventually brought her into the operation. She was sure he loved her because he trusted her enough to bring her in. She actually believed he was going to take her away from it all." Mali shook her head, her eyes finding Jake's. "She was jealous of us and the love we share, and I think she was lonely. Jeff took advantage of that." Turning her head, she looked at Felix and Kirsten. "He was furious that she let you guys live and didn't hesitate to shoot. It was horrible."

"She got what she deserved, as far as I'm concerned," said Kirsten, scowling.

At the lull in the conversation, Sword said, "I got to use my 3D Ninja stars." He grinned from ear to ear.

"No kidding!" Felix exclaimed.

Sword nodded. "Armano had Mali and was holding her against him with a syringe full of fentanyl next to her neck–"

Kirsten gasped, her hand moving to her throat. "Oh God!"

"And she used her fingers to let Jake and I know that there were two guards behind us. When all hell broke loose, I pulled them out of my boot and nailed 'em."

Felix grinned. "Cool!"

"What about Armano?" asked Kirsten.

Pointing to Jake, Matey joined the conversation. "Pirate here slammed into Armano but not before the needle of the syringe scraped Hoop's upper arm. I swear that flames came out of his nose." Everyone laughed at Jake, who shrugged, smiling. "The syringe flew away and they both went down. After trading punches, Armano got his hands on the syringe. By that time, we heard the sirens and when Jake told him it was over, Armano charged him like a bull." He put a finger on each side of his head and lowered it, imitating a bull. Everyone laughed again. "Pirate sidestepped him, like a true matador, grabbed the syringe and jammed it into Armano's neck. Armano dropped like a rock and was dead in sixty seconds."

Everyone stared at Matey as he told the story, transfixed, Mali included. She shivered, not realizing that Jake had come so close to death. Blinking rapidly, she glanced up and saw him staring at her. He winked, before turning his attention to the agent who had asked a question.

Fifteen minutes later, Matey and Sword were loaded into one ambulance while Mali and Jake climbed into the other. The agent said they'd finish the debriefing later. Kirsten and Felix followed in the agent's car, who let them borrow it and said he'd pick it up later.

The rest of the day was spent at the hospital. By four o'clock, the team was gathered together in Matey's room, who would be remaining in the hospital for a day or two for a few more tests to ensure there was no internal bleeding. The rest of the team would be released shortly.

The events of the day were on all the networks. While they waited for discharge, they watched the national news.

"...and the total number of people arrested, at this point, is seventy-nine." The reporter stared into the camera. "In case you're just joining us, in a joint effort and tipped off by an anonymous caller, the FBI and DEA have shut down the candy app, known as Dandy Candy, and the illegal drug operation behind it."

The cries of foul were quick and loud by everyone when the reporter mentioned an anonymous caller.

"Bullshit," said Sword.

Kirsten grimaced. "You're kidding, joint effort?"

"Anonymous, my ass," cried out Felix, causing the others to laugh.

"Shhhhh," said Mali. "She's continuing."

"...and can now prove that the recent fentanyl-related deaths in New York City, California, Colorado, and Las Vegas were all tied to the Dandy Candy app. The leader of the Los Rinches cartel was killed by operatives, and a local FBI agent was killed as well. It's unknown what her involvement was at this time." She shook her head, glancing at the co-anchor sitting next to her. "It's going to take a long time to figure all of this out, Bob. We are certainly fortunate that those two agencies cracked this months-long case involving the candy app, a drug cartel, and a fentanyl lab in Nevada. In other news..."

Jake flipped off the television.

"Are you kidding me?" asked Kirsten. "*They* didn't crack the case, we did."

"We could hardly tell the networks that rogue FBI agents cracked it, now could we?" Six pairs of eyes shot to the door. Special Agent-in-Charge Hernandez leaned against the door frame, arms crossed.

* * *

"Imagine my surprise," she began, arms crossed and looking at each team member sternly, "when I found out that almost the entire team at the warehouse was missing. Two of you were on a leave of absence and were told to stay out of this case." She turned narrowed eyes on Jake and Mali. "One person is supposed to be home sick, the mysterious illness apparently affected another team member, and a fifth person went AWOL."

Everyone had tensed up, as did Matey and Sword even though they didn't work for the agency.

"Special Agent Hernandez…"

Agent Hernandez held up her hand, signaling Jake to stop. "Relax. You still have your jobs, for the moment." She took a deep breath then walked into the room, closing the door behind her. Turning her head, she spotted Sword and Matey. "Ben Williams and Tim Jackson, I presume?" Both men nodded. "The Vegas FBI office briefed me during my flight, but I will obviously need a full debriefing from each of you." She settled into a chair that Jake offered her. "You should all be fired for disobeying my direct orders. . ." Again, she regarded Jake and Mali, then turned her gaze to Kirsten and Felix. ". . .for lying about being sick, and for pursuing an unauthorized case. While not unprecedented, your actions speak louder than words to me and have me wondering if we'll be able to work together in the future. Trust, once broken, is hard to repair, and if I can't trust my orders to be followed…" She trailed off.

The room was silent, except for the beep of the monitor still attached to Matey.

Hands on her knees, she appeared to be deep in thought. Finally, she leaned forward. "By the same token, I also showed a certain level of distrust by not believing you could do your job after what happened to your father." She looked up at Jake. "Nor did I take into account everything your team had been through in the past, resulting in a group of people who work together seamlessly. I apologize for that."

"If I may?" asked Jake. Agent Hernandez nodded. "I knew what I was risking, we all did. But we believed that no one was better equipped to handle this case..."

"...which proved to be true."

Jake nodded. "Yes, but you were right about my emotional state. Losing my father is something I'll have to come to terms with. Solving this case and taking Armano down was a big step in that direction. All that being said, we still disobeyed your order and, for that, I apologize."

The rest of the team nodded and murmured apologies.

Agent Hernandez smiled her thanks. "Now, tell me what happened, from the moment I put you on a leave of absence to the events of today." She leaned back in the chair and turned her attention to Jake.

There was a collective sigh of release as Jake started the debriefing. Each team member interjected their thoughts and what they witnessed as they progressed through the timeline.

Ninety minutes later, Agent Hernandez shook her head and stood. "The depravity of so many never ceases to boggle my mind. You've made a big dent today in the drug market. Congratulations on a job well done."

A nurse walked in, stopping when she noticed all the people. "Excuse me, but I need to check Mr. Jackson's vitals then we're taking him for more tests.

"We were just finishing," said Agent Hernandez.

"Can you give us a few minutes?" The nurse nodded then turned and walked out the door. "I will have to place letters of reprimand in your files, but they will be mild and will be offset by the success you had in bringing down the largest fentanyl lab in U.S. history. We will chalk this up to not knowing each other well, since I only recently took over for Frank Grant." She studied each agent briefly before sighing. She glanced at her watch. "Today is Tuesday. I need a couple of days to deal with Jeff Cink and wrap things up with the local office. The jet is flying out on Friday. I expect all of you to be on that jet with me and to return to work on Monday. I'll text you the departure information. Get some rest." She walked out of the room without another word.

CHAPTER TWENTY-FIVE

Weehawken, New Jersey
Eighteen months later…

MALI, JAKE, AND Heather sat on chairs next to a podium on a raised platform. In front of them were multiple rows of chairs where more than eighty people sat beneath large white canopies that offered shade. Various networks were positioned behind and along the outer edges of the guests. The sun shone brightly and, despite it being summer, a gentle breeze kept the morning cool. Mali's parents, along with her sisters and their families, sat in the first row. Sara and her family, Kirsten and Jen, and the rest of the team sat in the second row with Jerry's friends, Paul and George.

"Thank you, everyone, for coming out on this beautiful New Jersey day." The mayor, a jovial man, stood at the podium and addressed the crowd. "We are all here to celebrate the grand opening of the Gerald Black Fresh Start Foundation. When Jake and Mali approached me almost eighteen months ago with their desire to purchase this property and told me of their plans for it,

I eagerly jumped on board. They turned sixty acres of unused commercial property into this oasis for veterans and first responders. And while I am not going to describe the facilities behind us, that is for the Blacks to do, I will say that the city of Weehawken is grateful to them. They are not only helping those in need of these services, but they are also employing more than fifty veterans and professionals, with many more offering their services free of charge to the foundation. I believe you will all be as excited about this concept as I am. Personally, I hope it will expand to many communities across the United States. But that is for another time." He chuckled. "Without further ado, I would like to introduce Jacob Black."

The crowd clapped as Jake stood and walked to the podium. He shook the mayor's hand and thanked him before facing the crowd.

"Good morning, and thank you for coming." He took a deep breath. "Just over eighteen months ago, my father, Gerald Black, was killed by a fentanyl overdose. A box of chocolates laced with the drug was delivered to him while my wife and I were on our honeymoon. The details of why the chocolates were sent to him are irrelevant. What is important is that his death put Mali and I on a path that led us to where we are today. But we had much to learn. Fentanyl is a dangerous drug that has poured into this country via our southern border. It is mixed with oxycodone and other pain meds and passed off as the real thing, and people are overdosing. Cocaine and other drugs are laced with it, hooking addicts and recreational users alike on fentanyl rather than the other drug. The smallest amount, roughly four grains of salt, can kill an adult."

His gaze moved around the crowd as he spoke. "And now, candy is being laced with this deadly drug. Children are eating gummy bears and lollipops and are dying. Just after my father passed, there were multiple deaths due to drugged candy. Veterans were even given candy in California, not out of an act of kindness, but as a prank for a game to see who ate the drugged candy and who didn't. Most of the candy at that time was sold through an app, called Dandy Candy, and I'm happy to say that app is forever gone." The crowd clapped.

"But drug dealers are still selling drugs through apps like SnapChat, TikTok, Instagram, and others, using emojis of all things. I couldn't believe that when I first heard it." He shook his head, pausing to sip some water. "It's important for parents to be aware of what their kids are doing on social media. While drugs can still be purchased through apps, I am hopeful knowing that those organizations are exercising more diligence in tracking the sales and working with the DEA to put an end to this epidemic. And it IS an epidemic that we ALL must work to end."

Taking another sip of water, he glanced at Mali and Heather. Mali smiled and Heather gave him a thumbs up. "My dad was a policeman in Weehawken all his adult life. He loved helping people and fighting to keep Weehawken safe. While veteran drug use and homelessness have slightly declined over the past few years, it is still a serious problem. To honor my dad and all veterans, of which I am one, we decided to create this foundation and facility to help them overcome their addiction and get their lives back on track, to have a fresh start." He paused. "I'd like to introduce my wife, Mali, who is going to explain how the facility will operate. Afterward, we'll take you inside for some food and drink, as well as tours of the property. The day is yours to explore and ask questions. Mali?"

Everyone clapped again then chuckled when a very pregnant Mali struggled to stand. The chairs on the stage had no arms and she had nothing to assist her. Taking three strides to reach her, Jake helped her stand.

Waddling to the stage wearing an emerald green maternity dress and low nude-colored heels, Mali gripped the podium and smiled. "Whew! I feel like a duck, and probably look like one too. Don't be surprised if I start quacking." The crowd burst into laughter. "Thank you for coming today. We have worked so hard the last eighteen months to make this dream a reality, in more ways than one." She pointed to her belly, which sent the crowd into more peels of laughter.

She laughed as well before taking a few deep breaths. "This dream would not have been possible without the generosity of countless people, many whom I want to thank before continuing." She proceeded to thank the mayor, her parents and other investors, the medical professionals who would be working with them as well as Alcoholics Anonymous, the VA, and other organizations who would be involved.

"As Mayor Grayson told you, we purchased these sixty acres almost eighteen months ago, after leaving the FBI, and turned it into the oasis you see today." She spread her arms indicating the lush landscaping that surrounded the building behind her. "In addition to this building, we have two other large buildings, as well as two workshops, a barn with corrals for the six horses on site, an on-site all-purpose type of store, walking trails, and much more. The entire sixty acres is enclosed by a privacy wall. The purpose is not to lock anyone in but, rather, to provide security and to ensure the privacy of our residents as they recover."

She smiled as she spoke, the passion for what they created evidenced by her enthusiasm.

"We have taken a three-phased approach to tackling the problem of addiction and homelessness for veterans and first responders. The building behind us is the first stop for those who are addicted to drugs or alcohol, housing up to one hundred residents. Similar to the way AA works, they will be here for thirty days to detoxify. As they go through the program, they will attend group and individual counseling sessions, they will learn how to recognize their triggers for turning to drink or drugs, and they will be given the tools needed to help them cope and choose a different path. In the latter half of the month, they will have opportunities to enjoy the private garden behind this building and will be able to shop at the on-site store occasionally. This is the most restrictive part of their stay here. We have medical professionals on-site to monitor them as they detoxify, and other veterans and first responders will work with them in the group and individual sessions, again, using the AA philosophy. The top four floors are the resident quarters with shared restrooms. The first floor is where the cafeteria, small library, counseling rooms, and medical facility are located."

She glanced at her parents, noticing their smiles of encouragement, warmed by their support.

"When the thirty days are up, the residents will begin the second phase of their fresh start and will move to the second building. The focus in this phase is to learn a skill, work on their resume, and get the training and assistance needed to apply for jobs. The two workshops on either side of the building offer training in construction where residents can learn a skill such as carpentry, masonry, plumbing, and tile work. As with the first building, the upper floors are for the residents. The first floor includes a cafeteria, four classrooms for learning administrative skills, like typing and data entry, and a laundromat for the resident's use. In addition, there is a full-service career center with advisors to help with resumes and everything else." Mali paused, sipping some water. "The advisors will assist each individual to determine their best path based on interest and prior knowledge. We are somewhat limited, at this point, in the training we can offer. But as we move forward, we'll adjust and adapt accordingly. This phase will last anywhere from three to six months."

Mali smiled at the crowd before continuing. "When training is complete, the resumes are finished, and the residents are ready to start applying for jobs, they move into the third building. As you know, applying for jobs requires having an address. We give them that with small studio apartments on the upper floors. The first floor contains their mailboxes, a cafeteria, a laundromat, and a large room with suits, shirts, and shoes in various sizes for them to borrow when they go on interviews. There is also a smaller career center where advisors will help them search for jobs and will follow up as needed after their interviews. Our hope is to place our residents in jobs within three months, and we are working with local businesses and builders to make that happen. The resident will be allowed to remain here for up to one year total, even after finding a job. We want them to have time to save some money so that by the time they leave, they can afford an apartment, more clothes, etcetera."

A few people in the crowd gasped. Mali nodded. "Yes, this is a commitment, right? On our part and on theirs."

"What a load of crap," yelled a man.

* * *

A gangly young man stood in an aggressive posture in the aisle at the back of the crowd.

Startled, Mali felt the tension of those on the platform as the crowd turned to look behind them. She glanced at Jake, who looked like he was about to shoot out of his chair. She shook her head and Jake leaned back, still ready to move if needed.

"I want to hear what he has to say." She waved the

security guards away. "Sir, if you would step closer?" She turned her gaze to a woman standing to the side of the platform. "Jessica, please take a mic to the gentleman." After he was handed the mic, Mali said, "What is your name?"

Putting the microphone up to his mouth, his tone was belligerent. "Julian Bishop."

"Hello Mr. Bishop. Why do you think this is a load of crap, as you put it?"

"You're talking about an oasis and vets moving from one building to the next like it's some sort of utopia, and they'll leave here all hunky dory making fifty thou a year. That's not reality."

"How old are you, Mr. Bishop?"

"Nineteen."

"Do you have a family member serving?"

He looked down at his toes before looking up to stare at her, tears in his eyes. "My older brother was in the Marines. He's been out now for almost a year. He's hooked on meth, tried getting help when he first made it home. Nothing worked. He's living on the street now in the City, strung out most of the time."

"I'm sorry to hear that. Does he ever contact you?"

You could hear a pin drop in the crowd. Everyone was focused on the exchange between Mali and the young man.

Sniffing, he said, "He calls me every couple of weeks, doesn't want me to see him so he doesn't say where he is."

Mali absently rubbed her stomach as she considered her words. "Julian, may I call you Julian?" At his nod, she continued. "We created this place, and yes, I call it an oasis, because we want our residents to be surrounded by beauty and hope. Life is wondrous and good, and our goal is to help bring them back to that belief. Is this a utopia? No. A lot of hard work has to happen behind these doors, and every day for the rest of their lives. It won't be easy, but it will be worth it."

"You're talking about a year and a half, maybe more."

Mali nodded. "If someone starts in the first phase, yes. It's possible for some residents to start in phase two. In that case, their timeframe would be less."

"How is anyone supposed to afford this? Even if I could convince my brother to come here, there's no way we could pay for it."

Mali smiled. "I'm glad you asked. Come up to the stage. Please." She crooked her finger. As he approached, she picked up a card sitting on the podium, stepped to the side, and moved to the edge of the stage. People closest to them, strained to hear the conversation.

"This is my card." She handed it to him. "I want you to give him this information the next time he calls. We will pick him up wherever he is and bring him here if he wants to commit to the program. He will always have a place here. All right?" He nodded. "Why don't you sit right over there," she pointed to the side of the stage, "while I explain things."

He moved to the side and sat down.

Mali smiled. "So, like Julian, you might be wondering how they can afford it. Well, it's free for them. The only requirement we have, starting from the time they move to building two until they leave the property, is to work here. We require each resident to work at least twenty hours a week when they're in phase two, and a minimum of ten hours each week once they find a job. Duties are rotational. Residents could be working at any of the first-floor spaces of buildings two and three, in the barn or in the vegetable garden, with the cows, or they could even be tending the chickens in the chicken coop and collecting the eggs. Did I mention we have cows and chickens?" A few people chuckled. "We have ten cows and twenty chickens. They will provide meat and eggs for us. From the time the resident moves to the second phase until they leave, they have much more freedom. When they're not working, they can walk or run on the trails, work out in the fitness center, or go to the barns and ride horses. If they don't know how, they can learn. We have wranglers on-site caring for all the animals."

She took a sip of water then continued. "You might also be wondering how *we* can afford it. We have generous investors who believed in this concept from the start. We also have obtained federal and state grants. Between those two, we were able to create this oasis and will be able to operate for two years. We continue to pursue grants and we have set up a means for the public to make donations to the foundation. But I have to say that, as rewarding as all of that is, what warms my heart the most..." she patted her heart with her hand, "...is how the community has come together. We have professionals from the medical and education communities volunteering their time as well as the trades. Businesses are donating office supplies and equipment and are waiting in the wings to interview and hire our residents. It truly takes a village and that's what we're building here. That being said, even though we have a capacity to hold one hundred residents, we are starting with a third of that. Once we have an opportunity to fine-tune our operation, and our residents progress through each phase, we'll be able to introduce more into the system. Our goal is to become as self-sufficient as possible to reduce costs."

The guests began clapping, slowly at first, then many stood to cheer. Mali bit her lip and her eyes watered. She motioned with her hands for people to sit when she noticed a few hands rise in the air.

"Thank you. I can't tell you how much your enthusiasm moves us. I know you have questions but–"

Heather jumped up from her seat. "Mommy!" Startled, Mali turned her head and watched Heather skip to her side. Heather motioned with her finger for Mali to lean down. She wanted to whisper something to her.

Mali's eyebrows shot up. "I can't bend over, sweetheart, or I might not be able to get back up." The crowd laughed.

Heather looked over her shoulder at her daddy. She spread her arms out to the side, palms up. "Hello? Daddy?" The crowd continued to laugh as Jake rolled his eyes then stood and walked over to them. He picked Heather up and she leaned over and whispered in her mother's ear.

The crowd grew silent, many hoping to hear what

the little pixie was saying. The only sounds heard were a few birds chirping and the light breeze rustling the leaves in the nearby tree.

Mali pulled back and stared at Heather in surprise. "Of course you can say something." Mali turned to the crowd as Heather wiggled out of her daddy's arms. "Our daughter, Heather, wants to say a few words."

The crowd clapped as Mali pulled the microphone off the stand and handed it to Heather.

"Hi! My name is Heather and I'm almost nine years old. I'm sure you noticed that my Mommy is going to have a baby really soon. Well, I'll tell you a little secret." She bent slightly at her waist and put a finger to her mouth. "Shhhhh. Don't tell anyone but it's a boy and his name is going to be Gerald Jacob Black, after my Papa and my Daddy. I have been waiting forever to be a big sister. It took Mommy and Daddy long enough." The crowd erupted into laughter, causing Heather to pause and frown.

Mali turned beet red and just closed her eyes, shaking her head. Jake chuckled and pulled her close to his side, arm resting on her shoulder.

"I am sure my Papa in heaven is smiling down on us today because of this cool thing Daddy and Mommy are doing here, but also because of baby Gerald. I miss Papa and wish he could meet my new baby brother but, as Papa used to say, those we love live within us. So I know he's here." Jake squeezed Mali's side, and he smiled as he gazed down at her. "Well, I'm going to say goodbye now before they tell me to stop talking." More people chuckled as she turned and handed the microphone to Mali.

"Thank you, sweetheart." Mali took a deep breath, gazing out at the audience. "Please join us inside. We're excited to show you the facility and grounds, and we're happy to talk about the fresh start we'll be giving our veterans and first responders."

Mali and Jake turned around and looked up at the building. Heather wormed her way between them and grabbed each of their hands. They stepped off the stage and walked up the path and inside.

* * *